THINGS COME TOGETHER

THE AFRICAN CARRIES THE TORCH

BY

LARRY GRABILL

WITH ETIM EDUMOH

AND VERONICA BASSEY–DUKE

BibleTheme
Publications
1438 Baylor Drive
Colorado Springs
Colorado 80909

Publications
1438 Baylor Drive
Colorado Springs
Colorado 80909

Acknowledgments

We conceived the idea of writing a novel with the title, THINGS COME TOGETHER, and wrote the first outline five years ago. Since then, through many drafts and revisions, others have helped us. The students of Grace Bible Institute and Seminary gave us insights into their various cultures in Africa. Pastor O.N. Ogbouji of Open Christian Fellowship Ministries was especially helpful in reminding us of African parables and their meanings.

Margaret Durfee, who lived many years with African people, gave valuable direction from her knowledge of anthropology and expertise in composition and the English language. Ruth Ann Stoops and Mary Grabill were also extremely helpful with their sharp eyes in editing. To all of these we say a big thank you!

We also want to express deep, heart-felt thanks to the Ministry of Education of Cross River State for recommending this book for use by SS1 - SS2 students in all Secondary Schools in their state. This recommendation was made after reviewing the book using the National Book Policy guide lines.

Larry Grabill
Etim Edumoh
Veronica Bassey-Duke

Preview

The church stood in the city, a considerable distance from the market. It was considered orthodox and had been brought here by the colonial missionaries. The locals had taken it up at the exit of the pioneer missionaries, and it was generally assumed that its doctrines had been maintained. The building was a gigantic edifice made of ancient bricks. It towered to the skies in the sprawling magnificence of a colonial master-piece and stood as a symbol of religious legacy.

People worshiped there every Sunday. It was usually filled beyond its capacity. No other church building had as much significance in the whole district, and it was undoubtedly the most popular.

The hymn flowed from the organ and the mouths of the huge congregation. Gradually, the intensity grew until it could be heard great distances away. Euphoria filled the church. Now, everyone was in high spirits. They sang heartily. It was a familiar hymn, known since long, long ago.

> Rock of ages, cleft for me,
> Let me hide myself in thee.
> Let the waters and the blood,
> From thy wounded side which flowed,
> Be of sin the double cure,
> Save from wrath, and make me pure.

The pastor, an elderly gentleman, rose to preach. He read his scripture, the ten commandments. "Thou shalt not!" he thundered as one by one he expounded with eloquence on all ten. The amens resounded from the congregation—many from sincere hearts. Many other amens came from those who took advantage of the opportunity to profess even though they did not believe. After all, the important thing was not what you were, but what people thought you were. These pretenders seemed totally oblivious to the fact that the omniscient God knew what they really were.

After the service, a group of men rallied around one who was proposing a committee be formed to establish rules of conduct to combat the moral degeneracy and corruption in their society. Some of those present declared their agreement. The louder and longer they denounced the corruption upon the land, the more ethical and moral they felt. The very act of becoming indignant at others' evil actions made their own evil hearts seem good, not to mention, that it was good politics.

Ekpe was there, but he said little. He had no use for empty rhetoric. He longed for the day when the hearts of his countrymen would be truly turned to God.

Part One

CHAPTER ONE

Ekpe's life began amid strange circumstances, in the village of Eniong Effiom. On this dark night, Udo Ikpok Eto had left his wife to go hunting, even though she was heavy with child, because the wild forest was calling.

When Eno's labour started, she was alone, and the night was far spent. Her screams for help seemed in vain, but God Almighty was directing affairs. Someone knocked on her door. It was her husband's brother, whom they called Ette Ifiok. He was the last in the line of her husband's siblings. He had heard her shout as he was passing along.

After entering and seeing the plight of his brother's wife, he rushed out of the house with an oil lamp into the thick of the bushes. Soon he was back with the herbs he had gathered, and with them he concocted a mixture. Eno drank it and shortly the loud and harsh cry of the newborn Ekpe was heard. Filled with fear, Uncle Ifiok ran off into the night for help.

He ran until he came to the Abia Ibok who was known to be a dependable and versatile medicine man. The Abia Ibok came straight to the young mother and made his incantations. He told both uncle and mother that a terrible thing was happening to Ekpe's father in the bush where he had gone hunting, and that the situation required quick sacrifice. Otherwise, death could occur.

The sacrifice must consist of one white fowl, a pod of

kola, a pod of alligator paper, a chunk of ndom[1], a bundle of broom, a bottle of palm oil, a bottle of manyanga,[2] five seeds of dry pepper, a bottle of ufofop,[3] a stick of dried fish, and two pennies. Uncle Ifiok rushed outside and soon found all of the items nearby, except for one. Then he hurriedly returned and found the remaining item, a pod of kola nut, under his bed. With much haste, he brought them before the Abia Ibok.

The medicine man took Eno out in front of her house and prayed for her. He directed the prayer to the ancestors (long, long dead) who had power over their descendants. Then he broke an egg and rubbed it all over her. He also gave little Ekpe and Uncle Ifiok the same treatment. Ifiok received this treatment as a representative of the father.

Now the Abia Ibok sat on the bare floor and cast his strings of cowries. He made some concoction in a calabash and asked mother and uncle to gulp it down. They drank it, twisting their faces. The taste was sharp, very sharp. When they had finished, he asked Ifiok to stay with his sister-in-law until it was morning and make sure the baby was bathed with warm water and put to sleep. Then the medicine man left, and Ifiok did as he was told.

---

[1] White native caulk

[2] Kernel oil

[3] Locally made gin

CHAPTER TWO

Udo Ikpok Eto had always come back from his hunting bouts at the first cock's crow. But today, even though the cock had just crowed for the third time, he was not back.

"What exactly could be happening?" asked Eno in an exasperated tone.

"Only the gods know," said her brother-in-law

"The gods guide him," she cried in a shrill voice.

"I pray so too," he answered.

She sobbed all through that morning as Ifiok tried to calm her fears. Finally he succeeded by convincing her that the gods of the land would not let them down. Moreover, the Abia Ibok had done a thorough job that night, and his medicine was genuine. It had always worked. At length, Ekpe's mother stopped crying. She wiped her tears with the edge of her wrapper but did not leave her bed.

As day began to brighten, with the father still absent, Uncle Ifiok got up and went to his house. Finding his wife still sleeping, he wakened her and began to report the events of the night by announcing that Eno had put to bed. But before he could say more, Akon sprang from her bed exclaiming,

"What did you say? Eno has put to bed!" Then quickly tying on her wrapper, she rushed outside and headed for Eno's house. Popping in, she met mother and baby lying on the bed. The sight made her shout for joy.

"When did it happen?" she asked, lifting the little one.

"This night," answered the mother in a quivering voice.

Akon's shouts attracted nearby neighbors, and one by one they began coming inside. The house was soon filled with singing and dancing people. In their jubilant mood, they tossed baby Ekpe from hand to hand. Obviously they were not aware of the gravity of this situation.

One of the women brought a hot plate of Ekpang Nkukwo, dripping with oil. She passed it before Eno, but Eno didn't have the normal appetite of a woman who had just put to bed. Yet, as the women urged her, she forced the food into her mouth, though she could not keep it down. Nevertheless, the women remained joyful as they took away the dishes and washed them. But then Ete Etim looked around and noticed what the others had missed! "Where is the father of the child?" he asked in alarm.

Suddenly, the mood changed, and for a moment, silence fell on the room as everyone looked around. Then a chorus of voices began to rise. "Happiness has not let us notice his absence!" exclaimed the great wrestler, Ete Effiong, as he stopped chewing the long stick he had been using to vigorously brush his teeth.

"Where has Udo gone on such a fateful morning?" asked Mma Affiong. She was the Eka Iban, the leader of the women in the village. It was all Eno could take. She burst into uncontrollable tears. Everyone was stunned. Why would she be crying like this? When Eno could finally slow her crying enough to speak, she told of all the Abia Ibok had said, including the sacrifices he had made. Everyone reacted in surprise.

"How is it that none of us heard of this until now?"

thundered Eka Iban.

"I have been too distressed to speak about the matter," answered Eno amidst her tears. Then opinions started pouring forth in torrents.

"A search must be organized."

"This cannot happen."

"We must find him."

"Let's set out immediately."

"The gods cannot allow a bad thing to happen."

"Our ancestors forbid."

They talked at random. Okpo, the town crier, an eccentric who had no wife or children, took his gong and began to sound it forth to all the nooks and crannies of the village. It was a summoning of all the men to the Obong's palace. The Obong was the paramount ruler over the heads the Etuboms) of many villages. His palace was located in the middle of Eniong Effiom and consisted of finely structured mud houses, far superior to the other mud houses in the village. The reception hall was large. All cases were tried there, so it was held in high respect by the villagers. Bamboo chairs were orderly arranged in the reception hall and, in the middle, was a lengthy bamboo table.

The Obong was a very old bald man, precisely the oldest in the village. He often ground his snuff-filled teeth as he tilted forward on his esan.[4] He had four wives and over twenty children who moved about his house at random.

He sat on the huge chair in the middle of the palace. No

---

[4]Walking stick

one else dared to sit in his seat. He wore a tied loin cloth and a casual white singlet that had lost its original colour. As the young men gathered and began to chat noisily, the elders took their places on the bamboo chairs. They all vigorously brushed their teeth with long chewing sticks and spoke little, but when they did it was only in hushed and fretful tones. This, along with their bowed heads and the stamping of their feet in monotonous rhythms, signified their distress. The fact that they were barefooted was also a sign of grief.

The Obong got up, cleared his throat, and walked around. Silence fell on the house. Then he mournfully intoned:

"Eniong Effiom Esono O!"

"Iyaa!"

"Ibibio Esono O!"

"Iyaa!"

"Esono O!"

"Iyaa!"

"They say when you see a toad running in broad daylight you should not question it at all, because there may be something pursuing it." Immediately the men began responding to the proverb with choruses from their bellies. The Obong remained silent until the noise had died down. Then he began again.

"We only meet like this when something terrible has happened. And when we do, we gather to find a solution to the problem." The men concurred. "Our brother Udo Ikpok Eto is missing. The sun has risen fully, and he has not come back from hunting. What's more, his wife has put to bed a bouncing baby boy. We have many hunters here in this village. They always come back by at least the second cock's crow." The men concurred again, this time with a more punctuated, "Yes." The old men shook their heads in deep concern.

"Eniong Effiom Esono O!" he thundered, galvanizing his listeners.

"Iyaa!" they answered.

"We want everyone, every young man, to take with him, his gun, his machete, and every weapon that he has. We will go as a team, like a rope, to the thick forests to search for him. The rope-team will not sleep until the tortoise sleeps. We shall not sleep until we find him dead or alive. He is our brother; we cannot let him die like this. Let us all go out."

Everyone dispersed, carrying a feeling of distress. Something was surely coming upon the land of Eniong Effiom. Along with the present distress, other calamitous things had been happening in the village recently, and it was high time an appeasement was made on behalf of the land. But that was not the issue immediately at stake. *At least, the hawk must first be chased away before the chick can be blamed.* So every young man with blood flowing in his veins took up his machete, and every hunter carried his gun. As a team, they all headed for the forest.

* * *

While the search went on, the women remained with Eno and baby Ekpe in the house. At times her crying would subside, but at other times the tears would come like the gushing of the stream of Idimesa Udo-obong.[5] The women clustered about, trying to provide comfort.

"You are straining," gasped Ekaiban in feigned anger.

" I have told you that your Obot Emana[6] can never let you down, but you have refused to hear. I don't want to see you cry again."

The other women added their own words sorrowfully.

"It's okay."

"Don't cry again."

"I hope you know you've just put to bed."

"Never mind; he will be seen."

"Just keep on praying to the gods."

"Your husband is alive..."

Eno finally stopped crying, but she could not be comforted.

---

[5]A popular folk tale

[6] Nature god, or the god of creation, may not refer to the almighty God

CHAPTER THREE

Though the sun had risen to its peak, the men had not returned, and an ominous silence prevailed in the village. It seemed that ghosts were in command of the atmosphere, daring anyone to speak above a whisper.

Mourning for the dead was taken seriously in Eniong Effiom. The women would dress in black sac cloth and sit together outside with deep lines of sorrow carved in their countenances. When they spoke, it was only in hushed and fretful tones. Such was demeanor of the women now, but they were not dressed in black, for there was still hope. To be dressed in black could be taken as preempting the father's death, as though they were his enemies. This would anger Idimesa Udobong, the water goddess, and require an exceptional sacrifice to avoid her wrath. The wrath was almost irrevocable.

In the house of the newborn, Mother Eno was now asleep with baby Ekpe lying beside her, and the neighbor women still clustering round her. Their distress was evident by the roving of their eyes from one direction to the other and the anxious tone of their whispered conversation. In Eniong Effiom, as far back as anyone could remember, a father had never died on the day his wife delivered his baby.

The house was hot, and Eno was sweating profusely, so Eka Iban urged the other women to go outside. She would clean Eno and rub her with ndom to cool and relax her. Reluctantly, the women began to file outside.

"If we must go out, you too must go out," declared

Mmaiko, a tiny woman noted for her fiery temper and quarrelsome habit.

A few women chuckled, but Ekaiban was not the kind to condone nonsense from a fellow woman. She thundered, "Shut your mouth up and don't provoke my temper in this hot afternoon sun, or I will make you know your worth!"

Nobody spoke again, for Ekaiban was known as the most strong-spirited woman in the whole village of Eniong Effiom. In addition to her natural strength, which the people attributed to the remnant of her mother's strength, she was vested with the authority of imposing a fine on any woman who did not behave well.

When Ekaiban was alone with Eno, she applied the cool water and the ndom to Eno and the baby. Then, she stepped outside to send one of the women to prepare a meal for Eno. Soon the woman returned with a steaming bowl of otto.[7] They wakened Eno and set the food before her. She took the nourishment and a drink of water and then lifted her baby to her breast to quiet his crying.

* * *

The men had searched every corner of the local bush, and the sun was receding towards Idimesa Udobong, but they had not found their brother. Yet they were determined to continue looking until they found him. According to custom, they could not return to their village until they had found the lost person, dead or alive, even if they had to remain in the bush

---

[7]yam pottage

for days, weeks or even months.

Someone suggested that they should go to Ikot Ikwa, a virgin forest known to harbour many leopards. Some of the men protested.

"How can we go to that deadly forest?" asked one.

"Is anyone a woman here?" retorted another.

This ended their brief argument, and off they went toward Ikot Ikwa. They chatted on the way and sang ancient songs of war which their native warriors used to sing during the warring days when the villages fought for a place to stay .In those days men were really men of valour.

By the time they reached Ikot Ikwa, the sun had dropped out of sight. They had only their carbides to light their way. After some hours of searching, one of them stumbled over a trunk-like object. Then as he flashed his carbide on the object, he saw a human body and raised an alarm. The others rushed to the scene. Peering intently, they discovered that it was Udo Ikpok Eto.

His lifeless body lay before them, twisted grotesquely. The men stood there dumbfounded, and for a long time they could not say a word. *For what a fowl sees and shouts about is far smaller than what a goat sees while keeping mute.*

How could a full-fledged man be lying here in his own cold blood? What killed him? Had the gods grown angry with the land? Only a couple of months ago, a man fell from a tree and died. Unheard of! A bad omen! And now, before their very eyes was the corpse of a man who had been very great in the land, a great hunter and a force to be reckoned with. To make matters worse, this had happened at just the time his wife gave birth to his son. The land was fast crumbling. Perhaps they needed to consult an oracle to find out if some sacrifice was needed to atone for some misdeed. They were overwhelmed with grief.

They wrapped the corpse in banana leaves, dug a grave, and buried it there in the forest. It was taboo to carry the corpse home to the village. The whole village could be inflicted with very deadly diseases. After the burial, they went to the stream of Idimuko[8] and washed where men of valour were known to wash. Failing to cleanse themselves of the murk before they returned to the village could incur the deadly wrath of the gods. Finally, they began making their way home, but it was dawn when they arrived.

No one cried. It was taboo to cry for a person who had died in the bush, and even more so, when the cause of death was unknown. Even Eno did not cry openly, though she sobbed while hiding in her room.

She continued to think of her deceased husband until she became pale and unhealthy. The women gossiped about her condition, especially as they went to the stream.

---

[8]stream of courage

CHAPTER FOUR

Ette Ifiok took responsibility for the survival of Eno and Ekpe. He arranged for them to own a cassava farm so they could have food. He also provided the initial capital for Eno to develop a business of selling kola nuts, palm oil, alligator pepper, dried fish, and locally made gin (ufofop). Thus provision was made for their bare necessities.

As Ekpe grew he began to mingle with Uncle Ifiok's children. He ate with them and became virtually a part of their family. Yet when his mother called he would run to help her sweep and wash dirty dishes and pots. He also would have a taste of her meal. The saying held true for him, "No matter how much a child ate outside, there was still a difference in his mother's meal." Ekpe always had the warmest feelings toward his mother.

Ubong was Ekpe's favorite cousin and the two were about the same age. They became bosom friends and would often go to Eno's hut to get dried fish and the mouthwatering delicacy of meat smoked in palm oil and sprinkled with pepper and salt. Every so often, Ubong would whisper into Ekpe's ear, "Are you not hungry for some smoked meat?" This would be all the prompting Ekpe would need, and off they would run to enjoy the rich flavor of Eno's delicacies. On these occasions, the boys began to notice that Ekpe's mother was gradually becoming more herself. She was learning to cope with the loss of Ekpe's father. Yet she would occasionally sit and ponder as tears rolled down from her eyes.

The primary school the cousins attended was very primitive, but they were fortunate to have an unusually well-qualified teacher for a village. As a result, they got a good basic education of reading, writing, and arithmetic along with some history, geography, and a little science. They learned to read and write their tribal language, but most of their studying was in English.

One day, after Ekpe had finished primary school, his uncle called him into his hut. Uncle Ette was chewing kola nut with naked pepper and drinking palm wine. "Sit down," he said, pointing to the bamboo chair in front of him. Taking the seat, Ekpe held his head downward without looking directly into his uncle's eyes, for it was considered great cheekiness to look directly at an elder. A child who would do this was not liked by the elders. Ette was munching his kola nut steadily and fanning some air into his mouth to balm the hotness of the pepper, but he did not speak. The pepper choked him slightly causing him to cough, so he took a large gulp of his palm wine from his ukpok[9] and heaved a sigh. This prompted Ekpe to say, "Ette welcome." This was the way to address an elder when under these circumstances. To further show respect, Ekpe reached out and took the calabash from him. Uncle Ette waited yet a little while longer and then began to speak.

"Ekpe, Ekpe, Ekpe!" he called.

"Ette," answered Ekpe.

"How many times did I call you?"

---

[9] Calabash cup

"Three times. "

"That is right. *They say when a baby hawk begins to develop claws, it must learn how to carry chicks.* You have grown of age now and should start thinking of making a living for yourself and your future. So why have I called you? I have called you to hear what you hope to do for yourself. Is it farming? Hunting? Trading? Or something else? I want to give you a solid foundation now, for how should I give it after I die?"

What Uncle Ette didn't know was that the intelligent Ekpe had been doing a lot of thinking—perhaps too much thinking for a boy of his age. Various questions had been troubling him. Why had the gods of the land allowed such strange circumstances to accompany his birth? Why had the Abia Ibok's medicine not saved his father?

Other questions had also been eating away at his confidence in the beliefs of the elders. Only last year they had been in war with a neighboring village. An oracle had been consulted to know the war god's medicine for winning the war, and the instructions were dutifully followed. Yet their village sustained a humiliating defeat. He had also been observing that the idols never ate the food that was offered to them. If they were real and alive, why didn't they eat the food?

Worst of all, there was no satisfaction in all of these religious activities. The more one tried to appease the gods, the more they seemed to demand. After one had sacrificed his best, he still felt empty and fearful. Furthermore, Ekpe had heard of the Christian way. Christian beliefs seemed to offer hope.

Now Uncle's proposal seemed to be bringing that hope within reach, and the rebellious attitude that he had been secretly harbouring surfaced and took control. Had not Ette asked, "What do you hope to do for yourself?" He would speak his mind. "I want to know the Christian way. I want to go to a Christian school," he answered assertively.

The surprised Uncle Ette did not reply for a long time, and when he finally did his tired voice revealed his disappointment. But he was not the kind to force anyone to do anything against his wish. "If that is your wish, it will be granted," he said with an air of surrender. After all, he knew that many young men of the day were leaving the old way. He worried that the gods of the land would be angry.

The next week, Ekpe began to make preparations. He washed his clothes and gathered a few other possessions. Eno was greatly saddened. The thought of her only son leaving her to go to a far and strange land was too much, but there was nothing she could do. Ette had the authority since her husband was no longer living.

She gave her son dried fish, smoked meat, palm oil, and some money. Ette gave him amulets and talismans to guide him in his journey. A lot of sacrifices were made for Ekpe, by the Abia Ibok, for guidance and protection. On the appointed day, he gathered his things and entered a vehicle to make his departure. The womenfolk of his family cried, but they could do nothing to stop the young man. Ekpe was determined to go in search of greener pastures.

*   *   *

The journey was slowed by flat tires from the rough road and a leaky radiator, but finally the car arrived at the school compound. By then it was night, so the driver, named Boma, welcomed Ekpe to his house and instructed his children to provide him with water for bathing. After the refreshing bath, he went inside to meet a sumptuous meal of foofo[10] and pumpkin leaf soup. By now he had developed a voracious appetite, so he fell into the attractive plate of food with exceeding haste. The little daughter, named Ebitimi, stared in utter amazement and giggled until her mother scolded her. This sent her running into the inner room.

Ekpe spent the night on the creaking bamboo bed, tossing and turning with anxious thoughts. Tomorrow he would encounter new people and new ways. His head was full of speculation. He had heard that he would be required to walk on his knees, crawl on his belly, and accept a good flogging. Yet he prayed earnestly for the day to break so he could know what would take place. Finally sleep came.

---

[10] Fermented cassava

CHAPTER FIVE

The next thing Ekpe knew he was awakened by a call from his host, and day was dawning. He dressed and was given more to eat. Then Boma hurried him off to the school in his car.

When they arrived at the school compound, Boma took him to the office and introduced him to the man at the desk who peered at him through his glasses. Boma also gave the bespeckled man the necessary information for Ekpe's initial registration, and then Ekpe was taken to a dormitory that was crowded with other boys. There, he was shown a bed space which was to be shared with a boy from the east named Okonkwo. This did little to put him at ease, for he had heard of much friction between Okonkwo's tribe and his own.

The next day he was awakened by the terrible noise of a great iron bell! Quickly, he joined the other boys in getting washed and dressed. Then, he followed them to the assembly hall. Ekpe understood that they were gathering for prayer, but he was amazed at the procedure. Everyone closed their eyes. One by one, they began talking to their God as though he were just another person standing nearby.

What really perplexed him was that they seemed to be praying to one supreme God. Surely they would soon make a sacrifice of fowl or goat on the altar at the front of the room! But no—even though their prayers continued—they were making no moves to offer sacrifice or pour out libation to the ancestors. Their God didn't seem to require that. "A god who would not demand sacrifice must be a weak god," he mused.

Did these people have no regard for their ancestors? He was not sure it would be safe to live here. The wrath of the gods would surely come down upon this place.

Two other boys from Ekpe's tribe helped him understand the preacher's message from the Bible. The reason no sacrifice was required in their worship was that one man of long ago had given His life as a sacrifice. He was crucified on a cruel cross almost two thousand years ago. This brought an end to the need of offering animal sacrifices to God. This man, whom they called Jesus, was the Son of God, so His death was important enough to end all sacrifices.

If this strange teaching was true, his family and village were missing something very important. He pondered on why no one had ever told them about Jesus. He thought and thought about this until his thoughts hurt his head. Maybe this new teaching was all a big lie. He was confused! His heart got heavier and heavier.

Ekpe enjoyed the daily classes and he studied hard. He was determined to learn all he could and to make very good grades. Because he applied himself so diligently, the teachers all liked him and took a great interest in helping him. He also was well-liked by all of the other students. And in spite of his serious pursuit of education, he became known for his hilarious sense of humor. He was always ready for a good laugh.

Ekpe's interest in knowing about God grew as the preachers spoke in the assembly hall three times a week. But it was one particular message that really got to him. The preacher declared that God was angry with the wicked every day, and then he had the audacity to declare that hatred, covetousness, and evil thoughts were wicked. Ekpe knew he was guilty in all three areas.

That night Ekpe and Okonkwo talked for a long time about the sermon. Okonkwo confessed that his lying and cheating was troubling him. It had never bothered him before today's sermon. Craftiness had become a way of life for him.

Ekpe and Okonkwo also talked about Jesus dying. This was still a mystery to them. How could a loving God require His Son to die, and why would He be so angry about their lying and cheating? They both had been inclined to believe that this kind of craftiness was necessary to make one's way in life. These thoughts greatly agitated their minds. When sleep finally did come, Ekpe dreamed a grotesque spirit was about to devour him with its sharp teeth. His screams woke Okonkwo and the other boys. Needless to say, they got no more sleep the rest of the night.

The next day was Sunday. The morning meeting at the assembly hall was uneventful, but that night a guest speaker preached a masterpiece. He clearly portrayed, from Colossians 2:14 in the Bible, that a record is kept of everyone's wrongdoing in the memory of God. He thundered, "We will all stand condemned in his sight, for we are guilty of breaking God's law. We all deserve to be punished for our sin." Ekpe and Okonkwo were sure that this preacher had been standing outside the window of the dorm last night and had heard their conversation.

But then just as despair was about to overtake them, the sermon took a different turn. God had sent his Son to die for us so we would not have to be punished for our sin. Ekpe gave Okonkwo a glance. Somehow they had missed that point— that Jesus had actually died for them. He died to erase the record of their sin. Their sin would not be held against them if they would confess it, turn from it, and accept God's forgiveness. Furthermore, they would receive new life. They would be born again.

Suddenly, Ekpe began to sob. His heart was touched to think that the almighty God would send his Son to die in his place. As he bowed his head in humble contrition, he sensed that Okonkwo was also beginning to sob. They both felt mixed emotion—sorrow for their sin combined with great gratitude to God for sending His Son to provide salvation.

When the preacher finished his sermon, he invited all those to the front who wanted to receive God's salvation. Okonkwo went first and Ekpe followed. They both poured out their hearts in prayer to God, confessing their sin and penitently telling God how sorry they were for it. They also asked God to forgive them and to help them turn from the practice of sin. Suddenly, Ekpe felt a great peace flood his heart, and a few moments later Okonkwo felt the same. They now knew that God's record of their sinful acts had been destroyed, and they had been born again.

The preacher showed them 2 Corinthians 5:17 in the Bible. "Therefore, if anyone *is* in Christ, *he is* a new creation; old things have passed away; behold, all things have become new." As he read, the boys recognized that the verse was talking about them. Later Okonkwo and Ekpe concurred that the idea of being in Christ was a little hard to understand. But

Okonkwo expressed that he could understand the part about being a new creation because he felt like a new person. Ekpe replied that he felt the same and added that even the surroundings seemed different. The trees seemed more beautiful and the sky, though dreary as usual, seemed brighter. They both felt great passion for God and knew down deep in their hearts that they were Christians.

Later in the dorm, they marveled at the great love for each other God was developing in their hearts though they were from different tribes that often were at odds. This bond seemed to give them a preliminary vision of barriers between the Nigerian tribes being broken down in Christ.

CHAPTER SIX

From the night Ebitimi first met Ekpe, when she was just a little girl, she had been drawn to him. When her father later hired him to do the chores around the house she always made it a point to observe him. The twinkle in his eye and his fascinating voice made her feel bright and happy inside. She would watch from around the corner while he was washing the clothes in back of the house or sneak up behind him when he was ironing. When he noticed, he would smile and give her some joyful words. Then she would be satisfied and dash away to her play.

Gradually they became good friends, and she would help him carry the clothes to the back or bring him a drink. This was a little unusual because a servant boy was normally relegated to a status of unimportance and expected to fare for himself. But little girls do not always follow form, especially not ones like vibrant and spontaneous Ebitimi. By the time Ekpe had graduated from the mission school, a real brotherly-sisterly bond had developed between them. Ebitimi's three brothers had also grown very fond of Ekpe, but from now on they would see him less frequently because he was going to Bible College.

*　*　*

For Ekpe and Okonkwo, the courses in Bible College were very difficult because the books were all written by authors from American or European culture. These authors wrote of concepts that were hard for Ekpe and Okonkwo to understand against the background of their culture. One day, after Ekpe was finally beginning to understand the word, regenerate, he cried out in exasperation, "Doesn't the word mean 'to be born again?' Why don't they just say that? That is what Jesus was talking about to Nicodemus. I can understand 'born again.' To be born again is to receive the Spirit of God in you."

"You are doing some good thinking," declared Okonkwo, "but the Bible does use the word regeneration. It says that Jesus has 'saved us through the washing of regeneration and renewing of the Holy Spirit.'[11] And regeneration has a slightly different meaning than the term 'born again.'"

"All right, teacher. I see that the Bible does speak of regeneration," conceded Ekpe, laughing. "So how does regeneration differ from being born again?"

Okonkwo began, "The old life[12] that we had before we became Christians was a stream of water flowing from a polluted source. The source was selfishness. The farther the stream flowed the more polluted it became as it gathered more selfish attitudes and deeds, such as lying, cheating, stealing and fornication. To be born again is to get a new source of life —a different stream. The source of this stream is God and God is love. This love, which is not mere human love, works as a stream of water to wash the selfishness away. This washing is regeneration. In this whole process, *being born again* is the *cause*, and *regeneration* is the *effect* (or

---

[11] Titus 3:5

[12] The bible calls the old life the old man, Epesians 4:22

what is caused). This is the difference between the two.

"Good!" exclaimed Ekpe. "Now you are teaching like Jesus taught. He taught with earthly pictures. He talked about spiritual growth in terms of the soil and plants. He taught about bringing people to God in terms of catching fish. The people of our culture like pictures like this, and when we draw pictures with our words they understand.

"As I think about it, Okonkwo, I see that the culture of the Bible is more like ours than the culture of the scholars that write our books. This is why the Bible is often more understandable to us than the writings of scholars that try to explain the Bible. We need to spend more time studying the Bible. We cannot depend fully on the scholars."

"Yes, yes," responded Okonkwo. "And we need to look at the whole picture of the Bible, not just parts of it. We need to see all the parts fitting together like the concrete blocks of a house. It takes all of the blocks to make a complete house. Only when we look at all of the parts of the Bible will we be able to see the whole house."

"Well, you made your point again," said Ekpe. "We can't just look at the *born again* block; we must also look at the *regeneration* block."

"You are learning well, my brother," replied Okonkwo with a smile.

"You were talking about a stream of water and now you are talking about a house. Do you remember that Ezekiel tells in the Bible about the temple he saw that had a stream of water flowing from it?" asked Ekpe[13]

"I had forgotten about that!" cried Okonkwo. "The temple he saw in the vision was the house of God, and the stream became a mighty river that brought life. Trees grew by the river and fish grew in it. When the river reached the sea, the sea was healed, so that it was no longer salt water."

"Ezekiel's word picture puts your two word pictures, the house and the stream of water, together!" exclaimed Ekpe.

"Exactly!" declared Okonkwo excitedly. "And come to think about it, the Bible is God's *house* of truth. When we learn from its pages, we receive the *stream of life* that regenerates us."

"Right! You are so right! This word picture also brings to mind one of our proverbs, *The closer one gets to the source of the stream the clearer he sees it.* The closer one gets to the Bible the more clearly he sees God's truth."

"Yes, Ekpe, we can even understand regeneration when we get close enough to the Bible."

"Eh-henh! You made your point again. You are a mighty teacher. You keep coming at me again and again like the Bible says, "Precept upon precept, precept upon precept,

Line upon line, line upon line, Here a little and there a little."[14]

"And you are getting better at quoting the Bible all the time," noted Okonkwo.

---

[13]Ezekiel 47

[14]Isaiah 28:10

"Mighty teacher, since you are in a teaching mood, draw me a picture of faith. I know faith is one of the main building blocks of the Bible-house you were alluding to, but it is kind of abstract to me."

Okonkwo responded, "Faith can be illustrated by a baby resting in its mother's arms. The baby *believes* his mother can and will take care him, so he rests *trustingly* in her arms. This *belief* and *trust* is faith. Faith causes us to *believe* in God's power to provide for us, so because we believe in Him, we rest *trustfully* in His care. Faith doesn't worry about what food we will eat or what clothes we will wear. Faith also submits to God's will and acts with Him."

"Wait," cried Ekpe, "I am not sure I agree. I have understood that faith tells God what to do."

"No, that is wrong. Faith cries for God's will to be done. When we pray for something like praying for people to be born again, we are praying for what God has already decided He wants to happen. The prayer of faith simply gives God the channel to do what He has been wanting to do. For some reason God depends on our prayers, and He inspires us to pray according to His will."

"But suppose I want to pray for something, and I don't know if it is God's will to provide that something," protested Ekpe.

"First we must submit to God's will. We must be willing to accept whatever God chooses for us. Then God will show us His will as we pray. For example, a person may want a car, but as he prays for a car, God may show him that he doesn't need the expense of maintaining a car at the present time. Or,

God may give assurance (hope) that a car is coming. If this is the case, as the person prays for a car, God will give him a calm trust that the car is coming. The person will be able to rest in the hope that a car is coming like a baby rests in assurance that his mother is going to take care of him and feed him from her breast.

If one is agitated and feels desperate, it is obvious that he is not praying well. He is not praying with submission and trust. If one prays with submission and trust for a car, God may give him transportation from someone else's car. And this may actually make life easier than having the expense of owning a car."

"Well, Okonkwo, I must say this is different than some teach it. Even some of our instructors seem to believe faith is telling God what to do. Does not Isaiah 45:11 say, 'Command ye me?'" asked Ekpe.

Okonkwo replied, "Other translations of the Bible make the true meaning easier to understand. The meaning is 'Will you question Me about My children, or command Me concerning the work of My hands?' Also, the context of the verse shows that God is telling us to do the very opposite of commanding Him. The chapter is all about God telling us that He is in charge and in command and that we should not try to lord it over Him. Faith says, 'I put my confidence in God and pray that His will be done.' This is why Jesus taught us to pray, 'Your will be done on earth as it is in heaven.'"[15]

---

[15]Matt 6:10

"You are very convincing, my brother," declared Ekpe. I will accept your wisdom about faith, but you are not finished. You must now draw me a picture of love, God's love that washes away the selfish, old stream of life. Love is also an important building block of the Bible-house."

"I will try. This love is hard to know in our traditional culture. Of course, we know certain kinds of love. We know about sexual love. We also know about other human love— the love a mother has for her child and a brother has for his brother, etc.—but God's love is a much greater love. It is not self-centered, and it loves by choice."

"Explain."

By 'choice' I mean that God's love chooses to treat people like God wants them to be treated, even if they are not lovable. God's love also chooses God's will above one's own will even when the natural inclination is to follow one's own way. For example, it may be more comfortable to live with the people one has been raised with, but God may call a person to live among people of another culture for the purpose of teaching them about God."

"Oh, really?"

Okonkwo continued, "Perhaps that still leaves you a little in the dark. I guess the only way we can get a picture of God's love is to look at Jesus."

"There you go!" cried Ekpe. "Jesus Himself is the only true picture of God's love. He went about doing nothing but good. When He was treated badly, He did not return the same kind of treatment. On the cross He ask the Father to forgive His tormentors."

"He did make a lot of people angry though," inserted Okonkwo.

"That was because He told them the truth. His love compelled Him to tell them the truth so they would turn from their false ways that were getting them into trouble. As I think about it, God's love makes us love what He loves and hate what He hates. That means we love the truth because God always loves the truth and always hates falsehood."

"Yes!" exclaimed Okonkwo, "Now you are becoming the teacher and theologian!

Ekpe continued, "Love and truth are husband and wife. They are married to each other."

"Yes again," Okonkwo replied. "You hit the nail on the head. The Bible condemns those who have not received the love of the truth[16] and commands us to buy the truth and not to sell it.[17] People sell the truth for trickery, bribes, and lies of all kinds, and when they do, they sell life, because truth provides what is claimed for Kola nut. It is claimed, *he who brings Kola nut, brings life.* Definitely, he who brings God's truth, brings life. This is why Jesus said, 'You shall know the truth, and the truth shall make you free.'[18]

"Love, and the truth that love reaches out for, is what is needed in the land. God's love would cause us to turn from

---

[16] 2 Thessalonians 2:10

[17] Proverbs 23:23

[18] John 8:32

the empty teachings of the false gods that keep people in darkness and confusion. God's love would also give us a heart for people of other tribes, so that we would do unto those of other tribes as we would want them do unto us. It would remove the barriers between the tribes and cause us to work together for the common good of all. God's love would do more to cause *things to come together* for our society than anything else."

"Yes," affirmed Ekpe excitedly. I am thrilled about the prospect of God's love permeating our society. God's love would give us the mercy that is so greatly needed. I don't know about you, but it greatly disturbs me that we have no good way of helping people like those who get seriously hurt in car accidents. Everyone who drives by is afraid to stop and help for fear that someone will blame them for the accident. If we had more of God's love in the land, I believe we would find a way to take away the fear from those who want to show mercy. Many lives would be saved, if we could feel safe in helping accident victims rather than leaving them to bleed to death.

"The story of the good Samaritan in the Bible clearly shows that Jesus taught the importance of showing mercy to those who get hurt, even when there is danger involved. The Samaritan knew that there was great danger in helping the man who was wounded and half killed along the road. He knew that the robbers who had done this could be lurking close by, but he stopped to help the man anyway."

"You are so right!" declared Okonkwo. "We do have to recognize that the attitude of society makes if very difficult to help wounded victims. But if enough people became deeply concerned, a way could be discovered to keep those who want to help victims from being accused of causing the harm to the victim."

"This discussion has been good. We have discussed faith and love, and we have talked briefly about hope. Sometime we will need to talk more about hope. But that discussion will have to wait, because my head is hurting from all the hard use it is getting," sighed Ekpe.

"Brain exercise is good for you," laughed Okonkwo.

"Yes, I agree. But, *to be a man is not a day's job*!" They both laughed.

CHAPTER SEVEN

It was always an exciting time when Ekpe visited Boma's house, but today Ebitimi was especially looking forward to his coming. She was now fourteen. It had been two months since his last visit when she had felt that tingly euphoria when she noticed how handsome he had become. Never before had she felt such feelings toward any young man. It had been a new, special feeling that left her feeling grown-up and glad to be a girl.

Ebitimi also liked Ekpe for other reasons. He had always been more polite and considerate than most men. It seemed that most men viewed women as pawns to be moved about at will. Fathers bragged about the bride prices they would get for their daughters, and the women were always expected to do more physical work than the men. Perhaps these factors of culture didn't bother other women, but for Ebitimi, it was an annoyance. This was one of the reasons she liked Ekpe. Ekpe held women in high regard. Perhaps he was this way because he had been close to his mother and had learned to deeply appreciate her.

Suddenly her thoughts were interrupted. Ekpe was knocking on the door. She wanted to run to invite him in as usual, but what was this shyness that held her back? Boma answered the door and welcomed him in with an enthusiastic hug. "Sit down my boy. You are welcome!" he said. "Ebitimi, get this young man some mineral."[19]

Ebitimi slipped away to the kitchen. She couldn't understand what was coming over her. She had not even greeted Ekpe. Never before had she felt so self-conscious in his presence.

Soon she returned with the mineral and whispered, "Welcome," as she set the glass down on the stand beside Ekpe's chair. Then she felt her face heat up as she opened the bottle and poured its contents into the glass. "Thank you much!" boomed Ekpe. She turned to give him a winsome, shy smile. Then her face got hotter yet for she was sure that her face gave her emotions away, but Ekpe didn't seem to notice. "How is my girl?" he asked enthusiastically.

"Fine," she replied in a barely audible voice. Then with tightened vocal cords, she could only mouth the words, "You are welcome."

"Are you getting shy in your growing up?" joked Ekpe.

Again she gave him that winsome, shy smile but with even more embarrassment. Ekpe laughed quietly, but Ebitimi could see that he was holding back from laughing out uproariously. She fled from the room. "You never know what gets into girls," remarked Boma with a twinkle in his eye.

Later, Ebitimi forced herself to come back into the room and stayed with her family and Ekpe for the rest of the evening, but things were not the same. She felt as though she was bound with ropes. Yet she and Ekpe managed some

[19]Soda, the more modern tradition symbol of welcome

conversation, and Ebitimi finally brought out the needle work she had been doing to show Ekpe and get his praise.

The visit continued with Boma, his oldest son, and Ekpe discussing the many obstacles to progress that their nation faced. As usual for such conversations, they finally concluded that the basic problem was the lack of money. Their society's basic problem was poverty.

◉　丄　✳

Back in the dormitory, Okonkwo and Emeka were engaged in serious conversation about the same subject.

"Poverty is our number one problem," declared Emeka. "Most of us struggle desperately to manage one meager meal a day and a cheap dress to cover our naked bodies. Our children walk about with dejected looks, driving the reality of their hunger into our hearts. We are in constant fear that they will be caught with Kwashiorkor[20] and die."

Would-be moralists sound off all the time. I can hear them now as they rave, 'Bribery, trickery! Misusing money given to the church! Corruption of all kinds!' But many of the very ones that rave end up falling victims to corruption themselves because they get caught by poverty. How can we condemn people who are simply trying to survive?"

"But wait," cried Okonkwo, "don't you see that if we resort to corruption we become dependent on corruption?"

"Of course I see that, but if that is the only escape from poverty what do we do about it? I know it is wrong. I am not

---

[20] severe malnutrition in infants and children that is caused by a diet high in carbohydrate and low in protein

condoning corruption. I am simply looking for the way out of our problem."

"The issue is about cause and effect. *A toad doesn't hop in the day time unless something is after it.* The question we need to look at is this, 'Is it corruption that makes the toad hop, or is it poverty that makes the toad hop?'"

"I see your point. You are asking, 'Which one is the cause, and which one is the effect?' Corruption may actually be the cause of poverty rather than poverty the cause of corruption." conceded Emeka.

At this point Ekpe entered the room having just returned from the visit to Boma's household.

Okonkwo noticed him just enough to say "Welcome, brother. Then with intense concentration, he entered right back into the conversation to say, "Exactly! Corruption is the cause of our poverty. However, I do acknowledge that poverty provides a strong temptation to become corrupt. Every society has their temptations, but when we yield to the temptation to make our own way, instead of trusting God, our actions become the main *cause* of our poverty. Corruption is *the cause*. Poverty is *the effect*. Corruption is falsehood and falsehood breaks down trust. Trust and confidence are the foundation for any good economy."

It works this way. If I were to convince you to purchase a car from me by describing the car in an untruthful way, and —"

Ekpe interrupted, "What? A car! Come now, Okonkwo. A piece of cloth is more realistic. None of us have the money for a car."

"Okay, okay, I was just trying to illustrate. What I was trying to say was, suppose I deceive you about the quality of a product that I want to sell to you, and you buy it from me because my lie convinces you that it is a good product. When you discover that the product is worthless, you would make a decision to never buy from me again. Your confidence in me would be broken down, and this would hinder trade between us. The resultant loss of trade would cause both of us to lose the *benefits* we could have gotten from good trade."

"But how would a little thing like that hurt the national economy?" asked Emeka.

"The same act of dishonesty that people use in little transactions is also used in big transactions. It is used over and over again until confidence in the whole economy of society is broken down. You see, truth must be upheld and valued highly in order for prosperity to exist. Remember, "You shall know the truth and the truth will set you free."[21]

"Okonkwo, your teaching is good, and you are getting the reputation of a mighty teacher among us," said Emeka. "And I am beginning to see your point, but I am not sure you are applying what Jesus said about truth correctly. Was He not talking about the truth of salvation?"

Okonkwo continued, "I am sure that God's plan of salvation is the most important truth, but what Jesus said applies to all truth. All falsehood eventually leads to destruction. It is like a spider's web that the spider-like Satan

---

[21]John 8:32

continually uses to bind those who yield to it more and more. The only way out of poverty is to follow Solomon's instruction in the Bible: buy the truth and refuse to sell it at any price." [22]

"Okonkwo, you win. Now I see why businesses of other countries are reluctant to invest in a corrupt society. They have no confidence their investment will pay off. Truth has to exist for them to believe that they will get a good return on the money they invest. Otherwise they will invest their money elsewhere. They have to be able to know the people who receive the money, will not use it for themselves, and they have to be convinced that those who are paid to do a job will do it. However, I am still unclear on one thing. Why do some corrupt nations prosper?"

"That is a good question, Emeka. The answer seems to be that corrupt nations who are prospering are simply coasting on their past integrity. Falsehood has come and it prevents them from having even greater prosperity, but there is still enough credibility and confidence within the system to make it work. But eventually, if corruption continues to grow in a nation or society, prosperity will be destroyed.

Of course, we do need to keep in mind there are other factors involved for good economy: thriftiness, wise investment of money, and saving for emergencies. But as people begin to trust God's ways instead of their own ways, they are more inclined to learn financial wisdom also. God's ways are

---

[22]Proverbs 23:23

ways of truth which include truth about finances."

Emeka replied, "Yes, and when a society is known for its corruption, it has to totally break from the false pattern to regain people's confidence. It seems that regaining this amount of confidence is a mountain that is too steep to climb."

"Emeka, listen," Okonkwo objected, "It wouldn't take that long if a consistent pattern of honesty began to develop in one place. The pattern would soon be recognized by those who have money to invest, and the prosperity that followed would quickly be recognized by people of other parts of the country. Then, when it was explained to them that a consistent pattern of honesty was the cause for the prosperity, they would be quick to adopt the new way."

"Okonkwo, you, Ekpe and I can start this pattern by resolving that we will always be honest in our dealings. The change could start with us."

"Eh-henh!" enthused Okonkwo. "But we must start by being totally honest in our relationship with God. We must be willing to allow Him to shine the searchlight of truth in our hearts and show us any falsehood that we may be harbouring. If we trust or cling to false ways, our relationship with God will be disrupted. And this loss of relationship with God will keep us from trusting God's truthful ways in all areas of our lives. Living close to God causes us to trust both God and truth."

"You're right. I am inclined to think God has some things to talk to me about, but I am willing to listen. I intend to keep my heart open to the searchlight of His truth, and as He shows me false patterns, I intend to ask Him to help me correct them."

"God bless you, Emeka, and I commit myself to the same resolution. This will allow a stream of truth to flow that will have a cleansing effect on our society," declared Okonkwo. Ekpe had not been saying much, but now he also expressed his agreement. However, Emeka and Okonkwo noticed a little less enthusiasm on his part than they normally expected from their spirited brother in the Lord.

Ekpe really was not lacking in desire to support the resolution. He was preoccupied. His thoughts were on Ebitimi. He had always been aware of her sweetness, but today it had attracted him in a way that was new. Also, he had caught some sense of what Ebitimi was feeling for him. Was this the beginning of something important—something that could lead to romance?

CHAPTER EIGHT

Just as Okonkwo, Ekpe, and Emeka were concluding their discussion, Adeyemi and Musa popped in. They were engrossed in a heated argument that began in the Bible class they had just come from.

"I agree that one should not deliberately worship Ogun the god of iron and Shango the god of thunder," said Adeyemi, "but if a chief of my clan becomes a Christian, he has a problem. To be a chief, he must perform certain rites. And I know that these rites traditionally allude to ancestral worship, but one can perform the rites with no reference to such worship. After all, a chief can have a lot more influence on people, to turn them to the true God, than one who is not a chief. And you know that if a chief refuses to perform the rites, he forfeits his chieftaincy.

The chief of my village is facing this dilemma. He has recently become a Christian, and he has been warring in his mind about performing the traditional rites. But I believe he has come to the conclusion that since the gods of the land cannot overcome the true God anyway, it is not hurting God's cause to perform the rites."

"Adeyemi, you know better than that!" cried Musa, "The Bible says in 2 Corinthians 6, 'Do not be unequally yoked together with unbelievers. For what fellowship has righteousness with lawlessness? And what communion has light with darkness? And what accord has Christ with Belial? Or what part has a believer with an unbeliever? And what agreement has the temple of God with idols? For you are the temple of the living God.' Fetish ways cannot be incorporated into Christianity. Jesus says 'Narrow is the gate and difficult is the way which leads to life.'"

"If you are so good at memorizing scripture, why don't you memorize what Paul said? He said something like this, 'If someone invites you to a meal that has been offered to idols, you should eat whatever is set before you, asking no question for conscience's sake.'"

"There you go again distorting the Bible. Before the apostle Paul said what you are trying to quote, he made it plain that if one knew the meal had been offered to idols, he should not partake. The inference is plain that to eat, knowing it had been offered to idols, would be testifying to having confidence in idols. Everyone knows that the fetish rites are connected to ancestor and idol worship, so a Christian cannot partake of these rites without suggesting he has confidence in the idols."

"Come now, I am sure that Ekpe would tell you that Christianity has gained prominence in his tribe by incorporating just enough of the teachings of the Ekpe and Ebongo cult to make it less offensive. Christianity is quite a drastic change for our people. You have to introduce Christianity in stages. Otherwise it is like pouring cold water on one who has just stepped out of a hot shower. Musa, just be honest with yourself, it is your Muslim upbringing that makes you so dogmatic on this. I am not so sure you are totally converted from the teachings of Allah."

This was the wrong thing to say, and before Musa knew what was happening, he flew into a rage. Charging recklessly at Adeyemi, he gave him a thunderous slap across the face. Suddenly, everything was deathly quiet. Adeyemi stared at Musa in bitter anger. Then he swiftly turned and hissed at Musa as he stalked from the room.

The sense of shame in the room was as thick as cold palm oil. Why should young men studying to be preachers come to this. Such actions were a grim reminder of the bitterness that divided Christians on this issue. Everyone sat there stunned, including Musa. Then Musa burst into tears. "I am sorry friends," he said. "I must find Adeyemi and beg his forgiveness."

After Musa left, Okonkwo said to Ekpe, "Is it true that Christianity has gained prominence among your people by mixing with your native religion?"

"No, I don't think so. Has it gained acceptance? Yes. But when Christianity mixes with the old religion it loses its potency. Such Christianity has no power to make a difference, so people just take it as a divergent form of the old Ekpe and Ebongo cult. They don't convert at all."

"That is what I thought, Ekpe. And really, if Christianity mixes with false teaching it ceases to be Christianity. Christianity does not allow for compromise, it demands complete repentance from the old life, including all other gods. Certainly Christianity cannot condone any form of idol worship."

"You are one hundred percent correct," inserted Emeka. "Yet the issue that Adeyemi is dealing with is an issue that needs to be looked at. There should be a way that a chief who converts to Christianity can retain his chieftaincy, because, as the headman of the village, he commands great respect and can wield powerful influence. Certainly, this would be a great asset in bringing others to Christ."

"I agree. We really do need to give this issue some thought," said Ekpe.

"Yes, I agree also. We really do need to give it some serious thought," concurred Okonkwo.

CHAPTER NINE

As usual, Ekpe was delighted to be back in his village for the long break between semesters in the rainy season. His mother's meal was still the best, and it was great to feel the welcome from Uncle Ette and Ubong. His family always treated him like royalty. They were proud to know that he was acquiring a university education. This fact alone lifted the status of his family and the entire village. For this reason, he was always the center of attention when he returned, even though many in the village did not wholeheartedly support his newfound faith. The fear of the gods of the land still had its hold on them.

When he first arrived, everyone was full of questions. It took about three days of painstaking, detailed answers to get the barrage of questions to subside, but the honor of it all made him feel important. Eventually, the conversations turned to what had been going on in the village. Many were full of talk about Ene.

Ene had been away to the city for two years, but since his return he had been promoting the idea that God wanted to deliver the village from poverty. He also had a strong message of healing. He contended that God wanted to heal everyone of their physical diseases. Ekpe was delighted that Ene was talking about the Lord, for he had been praying earnestly for the people of his village. Yet it seemed kind of strange that Ene made no effort to come see him.

The next day Ekpe found Ene in an animated conversation with the Etubom[23] in the center of the village. "God has a plan to deliver us all from our present poverty," he was saying to the attentive chief. "I want to call all of the people together and speak to them about God's plan. I will pray for deliverance for all who come. You will see our farms yield tenfold more than they have been. Our trade will bring much larger profits, and our barren women will give birth."

The Etubom replied. "I am afraid that the gods of the land will not like this. If they become angry with this new god, a curse will come instead of a blessing."

"Have the gods of the land been concerned with bringing us prosperity? Don't you see the sad state of affairs that we are in? We need to have courage to break with our past and give the true God a chance."

"I shudder to hear you say that. I cannot keep you from gathering the people together if they choose to come, but I cannot give you my blessing. I must regard the ancestors and the gods of the land."

"Then I understand that you are not totally against me, and I will send the word around. We must be delivered from our present state of affairs," declared Ene, and with that he turned to Ekpe. "Welcome! Welcome, brother. It is good to have you back in the village. You have heard of my plan, and I am sure that you will join me in rallying your clan for deliverance. First, we will have a meeting in my father's place. We will discuss having a crusade here in the middle of

---

[23] The head of the village

the village. I was hoping that the Etubom would back a crusade meeting for this purpose, but the old ones are slow to change."

"You will surely be preaching a message of repentance—calling for our people to confess their sin to God and turn from their sin as they trust Jesus to be their Savior?"

"Ekpe, you have always been the kind of person to get caught with details. We don't want to overwhelm our people with teachings they don't understand. I am quite sure that the Bible college you attend is pressing the matter of sin too much. What our people can relate to is the material plight they are in. They will understand deliverance from poverty, sickness, crop failures, and barrenness. They are used to crying to the ancestors for deliverance from these afflictions. In time we can talk to them about your kind of salvation."

"But what profit is it to a man if he gains the whole world and loses his own soul?"

"There you go with your arguments from Bible college."

"Those are really the words of Jesus, my brother."

"All right, the soul needs to be delivered, so my message on deliverance will eventually get to the soul. My present message is that God delivers us from poverty. I hope I can count on your cooperation."

With that said, Ene stomped off.

* * *

That night Ekpe attended the meeting in the home of Ene's father. He didn't want to appear to be opposing Ene. It could look as though he were miffed because Ene was leading the proposed crusade instead of himself. Certainly he would be happy for Ene if he could agree with his methods and teaching. He was fearful that the crusade would hinder people from becoming true Christians. It had the potential to build up false hope that would later be dashed to the rocks. This could cause people to lose faith in Christianity. The form of Christianity that already existed in the village that syncretized the ancestral worship with certain teachings of the Bible was harmful enough to the true Christian message. Another false teaching was certainly not going to be helpful.

The course of the meeting didn't alleviate his fears as Ene promised many kinds of prosperity in fiery tones. Many of the people were favorably impressed. Ene was a man of enthusiasm, and he had ability to convey that enthusiasm in words. "Yes, yes," they responded as Ene challenged them to agree to support the crusade. Ekpe asked a question about the venue but held his peace for the rest of the meeting.

The next night the crusade started. About one fourth of all the villagers were there. The following night there were more. By the last night of the crusade, over half of the people of the village were in attendance. Every night Ene prayed in a very loud forceful voice for those who stepped forward to receive deliverance. Ekpe attended each night. Enthusiasm was so high he began to question his own judgement. Maybe he had just been jealous. He had learned from the Bible that often it is hard to know one's own heart.[24] Ekpe hoped that he was not just jealous of Ene's ability to lead. Maybe Ene was

---

[24] Jeremiah 17:9

doing something good.

The crusade closed with high expectations and plans were made to organize a church. They would meet in the open air until a church building was built. A rather large sum of money had been collected in the offerings taken during the crusade. From this a building fund was established, and a weekly salary was set to pay Ene to be the pastor. The plans also called for an offering to be taken each Sunday to increase the building fund and maintain expenses.

For a few weeks, things seemed to be going quite well for the church. When someone felt that the profit from his business had increased, God was praised. Every time a child was born the people jubilantly gave the credit to God. Okojie, a merchant, became convinced that his business was really prospering. He was the most jubilant of all.

The people of the church were certain that their farms would yield abundantly, but as the rainy season wore on it began to look like the crops were actually doing worse than usual. They began bringing their complaints to the services on Sunday, but Ene would pray for more deliverance and assure them that they should claim prosperity. If they would claim it by faith, God would have to answer. God would have to keep His promise. Ene did not clearly show just what promise from the Bible God had made, but he kept implying that God would be breaking His promises if the people of the church did not prosper in every effort they made.

Ene was clear on one thing; if the person wanting deliverance would give him a special offering, the prayers would assuredly be answered. By this means, he managed to triple the amount of his weekly salary. He claimed that the money given him would be a seed planted that would grow monetary prosperity for the one offering the money.

Yet the crops continued to fail, and the enthusiasm in the Sunday services began to wane. Then the attendance began to drop off. People were murmuring against Ene. But Okojie kept insisting that if people would have real faith then prosperity would come to them. He said that the problem was that they did not have genuine faith. He reputed the idea that it might be proper to question Ene since his predictions were not materializing. Ene had promised that his deliverance prayers would bring prosperity without emphasizing real faith as Okojie was doing.

Ekpe began to see that his misgivings about Ene's teachings were not unfounded. He also noticed, as time went on, that Ene never did get around to preaching real repentance from sin and faith in Jesus for spiritual deliverance. In fact, it was questionable that Ene himself had ever really turned to God. No one in the church had any comprehension of the need to give their lives as a sacrifice to God. The whole motivation of the new church movement seemed to be the selfish desire for material prosperity.

By the end of the rainy season, only half of the people who had started attending the church remained faithful. The crops were failing, and the Etubom was calling for extra sacrifices to the gods. The medicine man had told him that the gods of the land were bringing a curse because they were not happy with the new religion.

Just three days before Ekpe left to go back to Bible

college, Okojie came knocking on his door. Ekpe could clearly see by the look on his face that something was drastically wrong.

"Welcome Okojie, what is the problem?"

"I am not happy with our church," he declared.

"But I understood it was bringing you great prosperity."

"My sales were way up, so I thought I was really prospering. People were buying from me because my prices were lower than everyone else's. Actually, they were too low. You see, I was getting a lot more for the goods than I had paid for them, so I thought I was making a handsome profit. I didn't need to replace my goods all season because I had a big stock at the beginning of the season. Not buying from the distributors for this length of time kept me from being aware of current wholesale prices.

Today I went to the distributers to buy more, thinking I had plenty of money to buy even more goods than I had when our church started. But what did I discover? The prices have gone up so much that I cannot even replace two thirds of what I had. It means I have worked all season to now own less than I did. And to think, that Ene promised us prosperity! *A lie told in the farm about a great harvest cannot be repeated in the barn that receives the harvest.* Ene's promises are like the '*lie told in the farm.*' The poor harvest of my business does not allow his promises to be repeated. Furthermore, the gods of the land are bringing a curse on us because we listened to his Christian message."

To hear this made Ekpe realize more than ever that his misgivings about Ene's message were not unfounded. He would need to discuss the matter with Okonkwo. He was greatly grieved that a disgrace had come on the reputation of Christianity. He didn't want to speak against Ene, but he had to make it plain to Okojie that true Christianity was not what Ene made it out to be. He tried to explain to Okojie that we must trust God through the good times and the bad and commit our lives to him so completely that we willingly accept what God allows to come our way. "God promises to supply our needs, but He may want to use the hard times to bring us close to Him."

But this fell on the hard soil of a heart that had been programed to believe that God was all about material prosperity. Okojie was in no mood to think about full commitment to God, so the truth that Ekpe preached did not sink into the soil of his understanding. It was with a heavy heart that Ekpe returned to Bible college.

However, he was to find some respite from those troubling thoughts, for on the way back he stopped by Boma's place.

The happenings in his village had so occupied his mind that thoughts of Ebitimi had vanished, but suddenly there she was opening the door. This time she was more her old self, charming and witty, though a bit of shyness was still with her. It only served to make her more attractive. Yet she was too young, far too young, to be considered for a wife, even if she was mature for her age. Boma was not home, so Ekpe was soon on his way again to Bible College.

After Ekpe left, Ebitimi could think of little else than how much she admired him. She was pleased that this time she had not lost her composure. She had not known he was coming, and had not had time to build up a self-conscious complex. Her thoughts were absorbed with Ekpe's charming way and strong, muscular frame. She remembered the time when she was small and had fallen, hurting her leg. Ekpe had picked her up with his strong arms and carried her to the divan. Her body yearned to feel those arms again. She could clearly imagine that the sensation would be quiet different than it was then. Again, she felt the ecstatic thrill of being a woman who could respond to a man of charm.

But this was not all. In Ekpe she sensed a noble spirit and strong character. She knew that he was a fine Christian. This is what she wanted in a husband more than anything else. Oh, but how could this come about? How was he to know how she felt about him? And would he care for her, too? Many other women were out there—women that were old enough to marry. The thought that he might find someone else, before age could prepare her for marriage, threatened to drive her mad.

CHAPTER TEN

"Okonkwo, remember the discussion we had about faith and love?"

"Yes, Ekpe, I remember it very well, and I have profited greatly from it. I also remember that I wanted to learn more about hope."

"Yes," laughed Okonkwo, "I remember."

"Well, since my experience of this past break, I think I know more about hope—the kind of hope that is real hope. The great need of society is hope. When we don't have true hope, we tend to manufacture a false hope so that we can have something to cling to. To explain what I mean, I must tell you the sad news of what has happened in my village."

It took over an hour to explain all about the empty prosperity message that had come to his village. As he finished, Ekpe concluded, "The reason my village fell prey to Ene's distorted message was that they were so desperately in need of hope. Ene's promise of prosperity had no substance, but it did seem to provide a ray of hope. It spoke to their need, so they grasped for it. But it was a false hope, manufactured by Ene and the people he learned from, even though Ene may have had good intentions and actually believed what he was teaching.

To have prosperity we must seek first the kingdom of God.[25] By seeking the kingdom of God, we enter into God's

---

[25]Matt 6:33

plan for our lives. Prosperity comes with this plan, but it comes on God's terms, not our own."

"I know what you mean, Ekpe. Some who focus on material prosperity acknowledge this, but many make promises without strong emphasis on seeking first the kingdom. This not only builds false hope, but it places hope in the wrong source. The hope is more in the preacher who makes the promises than in God Himself."

"You are right, Okonkwo. A light bulb came on in my head as I saw people becoming disillusioned with Ene. I saw the artificial hope Ene manufactured was really hope in Ene rather than hope in God. Of course, he said that God was the one who would deliver, but the people didn't know God, so they trusted Ene."

Okonkwo thought for a minute and then said, "I believe you laid your finger on the real issue. The people didn't know God. This was their problem. As we learn to know God, faith arises from that intimacy with God, and this faith, in turn, produces true hope. We don't get hope by just claiming it. We get hope as our relationship with God builds trust in Him. Hope arises from faith because the Bible says that faith is the substance of hope."[26]

"Indeed, hope is the garri[27], but faith is the cassava that the garri is made from. You can't have the garri without first growing the cassava," pronounced Ekpe.

---

[26]Hebrews 11:1

[27]Garri is a processed form of ground cassava.

Okonkwo replied, "Very good, I like your insight. Love also plays its part. As we learn to love God, we develop a strong desire to place our hope in him. Like the ground grows cassava which produces garri, so love grows faith which produces hope. Love gives the incentive to build the faith relationship with God that produces hope."

"Yes, Okonkwo." That is because love turns us from the old polluted stream of our own ways. The old stream always focused our attention on things that lead us away from God. Godly love causes us to reach out for God. As we receive God and place our faith in him, we get the hope that we really need."

"Now I see why my church got embarrassed."

"What do you mean, Okonkwo? I didn't know that your church had a problem."

"Well, I didn't want to tell you, but my church decided that God wanted us to have a big piece of land that had a large assembly hall on it. We believed that we needed the building for a church and the extra land for future expansion. Therefore, we decided to begin a building fund. We were certain that God would prosper our people so they could give the amount needed for the purchase. We must have been correct in our thinking because the money started pouring in. We were really inspired to give because we all caught the vision of what a blessing this property would be. And the offerings showed that God was prospering His people so they could give.

"However, someone suggested that there was a danger of the property being sold to others before we could raise all of the money. Everyone got worried that we would lose our chance to purchase the property. I see now that this is where we began to let go of faith. By worrying instead of trusting, we began to take our own way. We decided to approach the owner about a contract for purchase. The plan was that we would offer him the money we had in the building fund and then sign an agreement to pay the remainder over a specified period of time.

"The owner agreed to take the amount we had in the building fund as a down payment, but he demanded that we sign a contract to have all of the remaining amount in six months. To do this we knew we would have to raise ten times as much money per month as we had been raising. Some cautioned against signing such a contract. They said that since God had been sending only so much money in a month, He might not choose to send in ten times as much each month. They felt that signing this kind of a contract would be tempting God.[28]

"Now I must tell you the embarrassing part. To make a long story short, we should have listened to the cautious people. We thought that as soon as we signed the contract the flow of money would greatly increase because we had claimed that amount of money for God. In fact, just the opposite happened. After we signed, the flow of the money started slowing up. Needless to say, when the six months were up, we didn't have nearly the amount of money we

---

[28]Luke 4:12

needed. We pled with the owner to give us more time. But when he saw that we had only raised a small amount of the full price in the six months, he lost confidence in our ability to pay. Now he is offering the property to someone else and is refusing to give our down payment back.

"What really hurts is that the owner is allowing the new buyers to purchase the property for the exact amount per month that we were receiving into the building fund, before we signed the contract with him. He would have agreed to the same terms with us, if we had simply told him that was the best we could do.

"Now I see that we should have listened to the more cautious people. *The tortoise says he will hang his bag where his hand will reach.* The cautious people were right when they said that we would be tempting God to sign the contract. Because we were impatient, we were trying to force God to send the money much faster."

Ekpe lifted his eyebrows and said, "Was it not you who taught me that submission to God's will is the first step toward finding God's will, and the next step is to trust God to do what is good for us?"

"Yes, I have to admit that is what I said. I should have raised my voice against what my church was doing, but I found myself getting carried away with impatience like many of the others. Impatience blinds our eyes from seeing God's way.

"Also, it might have been God's will for us to wait until we had all of the money before we agreed to buy the property. We will never know because we were worrying and being impatient and greedy instead of praying in faith to know God's will. We were trying to manufacture hope instead of allowing solid hope to build from true faith in God. Yes we tried to have our garri without first growing the cassava. Now it seems that our faith has been destroyed. All of the church people are discouraged."

"Okonkwo, don't be discouraged. If the people of your church will humble themselves before God and confess their sin of presumptuously trusting their own ways, God will forgive them and help them grow the cassava of faith again. This faith will be a more understanding faith and will build solid hope in God."

"Thank you for the encouragement. I will feed on what you have said. I will pray that my church will learn to love God enough to grow the faith that is needed to have the hope of church growth."

Part Two

CHAPTER ELEVEN

Ekpe had finished Bible College, and he was pastoring what remained of the church Ene had started. After Ene's promise of prosperity had not materialized, the people quit paying him for deliverance prayers. Also, the weekly offerings dwindled to almost nothing so there was no salary for him. As a result, Ene lost interest and even stayed away from some of the Sunday services. Finally he was asked to resign and he returned to the city.

The amazing thing was that a few of the flock began to read their Bibles as a result of the little instruction that Ekpe had given them during his break. They were convicted of their need. They confessed their sins and turned from what they knew to be wrong to accept Jesus as their Saviour. Then when Ene began faltering, they stepped in to take turns leading the Sunday service. Their knowledge was greatly limited, but as a result of their leadership the church survived. They met in an abandoned large house that had once been used for other kinds of meetings.

When Ekpe accepted their invitation to return to the village to pastor their little flock, they were overjoyed. They knew that he could have taken a pastorate in the city with a handsome salary. Since his coming, the church had tripled its size in just a few months. He was recognized as a good speaker and a knowledgeable man of God with a concern for his people. The people loved him because they were convinced that he was not in God's work just for personal gain. He truly had a heart for the people and for promoting God's truth.

However, there was consternation in the village because he refused to marry Nkese, a girl betrothed to him by his Uncle Ette and his mother. Amazingly, Ekpe had not known about this arrangement until his recent return to the village. He was shocked to discover that this had been planned when he was just two years old. The girl's father was the very medicine man who came to administer fetish medicines on the day of his birth. Ekpe could not believe that God wanted him to marry the unsaved daughter of a fetish priest.

However, in all of the history of the Eniong Effiom people, it was unheard of for a groom to decline marriage to his betrothed bride. This was a break with tradition that could attract the wrath of the gods of the land. Consequently, a great deal of resentment developed against the church. This resentment gave Satan an opening to attack the church, and the more he saw the church grow, the more he wanted to attack.

In the meantime, Ekpe had become convinced that God wanted him to marry. Therefore, he prayed for God to show him the right one, but he was not inclined to consider Ebitimi because he had always thought of her as being like a little sister. Furthermore, he had not seen her for three years, and he had developed some interest in another girl. But he was about to see that God had other plans in mind.

On one cool afternoon Boma and Ebitimi arrived in the village to see him on their way back from visiting a church in Owerri. Some one directed them to his house. Ekpe was standing outside the front door, and as soon as he saw Ebitimi step out of the car, his heart began to race. He could not believe how beautiful she had become.

Of course, Ekpe invited them to his house. Boma seemed a little more distant than usual, but Ebitimi beamed at all he told her about what God was doing in the village. He could see that she had matured into a passionate Christian and felt the same sense of mission that he did. Plus, she was more charming than ever with that touch of shyness that made her so fascinating.

For weeks he could not get Ebitimi off of his mind, and the more he prayed, the more he was certain that she was the one God wanted him to marry. Finally he took time off to go talk to Reverend Effong who had been his pastor while he was in Bible College. He felt comfortable sharing his thoughts with the kindly man of God.

They talked of the burden that Ekpe would be adding to his life in providing for a family, but they also were keen to observe that a good wife would a great blessing. Reverend Effong stressed the fact that Ekpe should be getting prepared to spend a lot of time nurturing a wife and children. He made it clear that it would be wrong to allow his heavy schedule in the ministry to keep him from spending the necessary time to bond with his future family. Ekpe took this to heart, but it only served to make him more anxious to proceed with his plans to marry. He loved the thought of having children to call him Daddy.

Reverend Effiong thought that Ekpe had made a good choice and readily agreed to start the traditional procedure of arranging a Christian marriage by talking to the Ebitimi's pastor. They parted after earnestly praying that God's will would be done.

This next day Reverend Effong fulfilled his promise to pursue the matter by going to find Ebitimi's pastor. He found him in his church office, and after considerable conversation, Reverend Dave agreed with him that the proposed union would be a good one. Later that very day he called Ebitimi to his office.

After exchanging greetings with her, he said, "Please sit down. I have something to talk to you about."

After Ebitimi was seated and had been given a few minutes to relax, the pastor began. "Do you have someone in mind for marriage?"

"No one has asked for my hand in marriage."

"If someone comes would you like to marry now?"

"Well, that depends on many things. I would be willing to be introduced."

But Ebitimi was troubled about something she didn't intend to share with the pastor..she didn't want anyone other than Ekpe. Yet how could she refuse the wisdom of the pastor's choice if he had someone else in mind. They visited for some time about the big step in life that marriage would be. It was a fearful thing to suddenly face the thought of making a life-time commitment to be a man's wife. She knew that this would involve a lot of responsibility, and if it should be someone else.... Oh! that was too dreadful to think about.

" Dear God, Let it be Ekpe that pastor has in mind!" she cried within her own mind. If he was the one, it was almost too good to be true. Yet, even if it was him, she wanted to be cautious. She had seen other marriages go sour...she needed to be sure that this proposal would be God's will in His own time.

They had prayer and a great peace settled over her. She knew that regardless of what would come of this, everything was going to be alright. Before she left, Reverend Dave said, "I will arrange for you to see the young man."

Ebitimi was with her pastor when Ekpe arrived. They both greeted Ekpe warmheartedly, but Ebitimi shyly kept looking at the floor as they visited. However, when the pastor asked her, "Will you marry this man?" she looked straight into Ekpe's face and said "Yes, I want to marry him."

Ekpe caught the spark in her eye and felt the jubilation of knowing that Ebitimi was not just complying with the pastor's wishes. She really wanted to marry him. He was also taken back by the fact she answered yes immediately. Usually a girl would ask for time to pray about the matter. Obviously, she had been interested in him and had already prayed about the matter.

At this stage, Ebitimi's pastor turned the matter over to the marriage committee of his church. They would initiate negotiations with the marriage committee of Reverend Effiong's church, who would represent Ekpe's interests.

A week later this committee came to Ebitimi's home with Ekpe. The chairman explained to Boma that they wanted Ebitimi to be given in marriage to Ekpe. Boma asked for some time to think and pray about the matter. Five days later he called for the chairman and told him that he was willing to begin negotiations.

Now it was time for Ebitimi's marriage committee to work with her parents to present a list of requirements to Ekpe's committee. This was done and then the two committees negotiated an agreement.

The bride price was N70,000, and considerably more was required for the food and drinks that would be offered. Because Ekpe was carried away by the thrill of marrying Ebitimi, he readily agreed without properly considering the amount. Only some time later did he begin to come to grips with the awesome task of finding the whole amount of the bride price. N70,000 was a staggering figure. He would gladly have paid a hundred times that amount, but the real issue at stake was not what she was worth, but what he could realistically hope to pay. Yet to have suggested too low a price would have communicated that he placed a low value on Ebitimi. It would have caused Boma to despise him. The high bride price was a dilemma that culture imposed. It kept many a man from being able to pay the huge price to marry when he was young and needed a wife.

In his wildest imagination he could only conceive of raising a bare ten percent of the amount from Uncle Ette and his mother. It was even doubtful that he could get ten percent from them because of their displeasure over his refusal to marry the Abia Ibok's daughter. Where was he going to get the rest of the Naira? The more he thought about it, the more agitated and fearful he became, until he was totally obsessed with thoughts of how to find the necessary money. This drove him to pray many hours daily about the matter, but strangely enough, the more he prayed the more his doubts increased.

Time was wasting. He must be on with his plans for the marriage, but how could he arrange it when he had so little Naira?

In the midst of this turmoil, who should appear on the scene but Okonkwo. Ekpe welcomed him into his house with the enthusiasm and desperation of one drowning. How reassuring it was to see his close friend. This was the very person with whom he needed to talk.

They exchanged inquires about their personal well-being and that of their families. They were comfortably seated with mineral to drink when Ekpe began to unload his frustration on Okonkwo by explaining his dilemma. "The troubling thing," Ekpe said, "is that the more I pray the worse I feel. I do not understand what has happened to my relationship with God. Why would He bring me to this point of being full of desire to get married, only to abandon me to this despair?"

Okonkwo sat and thought for a whole minute before he answered. "Brother, I believe that you are so agitated that you are not praying with faith. Rather, you are praying in the spirit of fear. Therefore, the more you cry out to God the more fearful you become. Have you forgotten that you need to commit your concerns to God? You have prayed your heart out, O'boy. Now it is time to sit back and see what God will do. Remember, we cannot move God by the shear force of our crying to Him. We need to rest in confidence that God, who has begun His provision, will finish it. I believe you may have forgotten that God desires to give good things to those who ask Him!"[29]

"Your words are a comfort and they give me instruction. I have been too agitated, but I am fearful that God's plan will be defeated by the forces of evil. You must be aware that we are engaged in serious spiritual warfare here in my village. Some people are cooking our future in a cauldron to bring curses on us. I am fearful that the evil forces of these curses are keeping the money from coming to me. This is why I have been so earnestly praying. I must take authority over each of these forces. If I fail to pray against any one of these curses, I fear that God's plan for me will be defeated."

"We exercise the authority for our defense against Satan by holding the shield of faith against his darts of evil. We don't have to know all the strategies of Satan and individually take authority over them to remain protected. We simply have to keep a conscious hold on faith and the other armor of God such as truth, righteousness, salvation, the gospel, and the word of God. This armor protects us against Satan's attempt to spoil God's plan for our lives.

"If we occupy our minds with trying to know and defeat each of Satan's attacks, we become exhausted both spiritually and physically. Furthermore, if we think that we have to be praying at the exact time of each of Satan's attacks in order to be protected, we can never rest. The key is to trust God and consciously keep in a spirit of prayer. As we do this, we will find ourselves praying regularly for a reasonable length of

---

[29]Matthew 7:11

time with true faith. We will also be at peace with ourselves and God and have time to do other necessary things besides praying.

"You are exercising faith for many things. As a result you are presently winning the spiritual battle on many fronts. Evil is being driven back and people are coming to God. But the battle you are in danger of losing is the battle to trust God for you and Ebitimi. Satan has gained some advantage over you in this battle by penetrating your heart with the darts of fear. You have lowered the shield of faith by failing to trust God. We are back to that simple matter of the cassava of faith that produces the garri of hope. You have been in danger of losing the hope of God's blessing in your life because fear has damaged your faith."

"Okonkwo, my eyes have been opened. You remain the mighty teacher. God sent you here because He knew I needed your objective view of my situation. Already I feel faith replacing the fear that has been in my heart. I am confident that God will supply the need. Hallelujah!"

"Praise the Lord!" Okonkwo responded.

"Hallelujah! I have the victory over the fear that was about to destroy me!" Ekpe declared.

"Praise the Lord!" Okonkwo said again. "Ekpe, I do feel impressed to remind you that Satan could tempt you to take a short cut to getting the money for the bride price. You must patiently wait until God's time. I believe Satan has more darts of fear. He also has darts of self-dependency that could cause you to take God's plan into your own hands. He may offer some solution that is not God's plan. Remember how the people of my church got ahead of God in trying to acquire property? Be sure to wait on God in this matter."

"Now you are being a mother hen. Do not worry, I will watch out for Mr. Devil from now on. As we say, *Any dog that barks at me will be eaten by a lion.*"

In some way, Okonkwo perceived that his friend might be too self-confident, but he said no more.

CHAPTER TWELVE

The church was gaining respect in Eniong Effiom village, much to the consternation of the Abia Ibok, whose daughter Ekpe had spurned. Esteem for Ekpe was growing as well. The people loved him and generally viewed him as a man of God. Ekpe's mother attended church regularly, and even old Uncle Ette attended occasionally. Many had given their lives to Christ and the attendance was increasing. The old meeting place was filling up.

Everyone agreed that a new building was seriously needed. Then one Sunday three business men from the city, who had originated from Eniong Effiom, were in attendance. Being Christians they were thrilled to see that the gospel was finding root in the hearts of their brothers and sisters. Their praises in the service were exuberant, and their amens to the sermon rang out strong and clear.

The next Sunday they were back and again added much to the service as the church members caught the spirit of their enthusiasm and spiritual fire. After the service, the men expressed that they wanted some time with Ekpe. Hearing this, Ekpe's mother suggested that he invite them to his house where she would prepare a meal. The men gladly accepted, and before the day was over they informed Ekpe that they wanted to provide the money to build a new church.

Ekpe could hardly believe his ears. Later arrangements were made with the bank in the city (which was only 20 kolometers away) to provide the funds as needed. The men had such confidence in Pastor Ekpe that they left the distribution of the money entirely to his discretion.

Satan was furious because the villagers were turning to the Lord. In doing this, they were turning from their charms and fetish ways. Some were even destroying their articles of ancestor worship. This hindered Satan from keeping them in the death grip of fear of the gods. His rage against the young church knew no bounds. He was determined to undermine and destroy.

He had no *direct* power over those who had committed their lives to Jesus and were trusting God to protect them. But if he could reactivate old fears like he had with Ekpe, the new Christians would lower their shields of faith. Then he could successfully make a direct frontal attack. Satan had just been ready to make this kind of an attack on Ekpe when Okonkwo showed up and spoiled his plans. Satan was determined to try again.

He would try from a different angle this time. Satan didn't like to come against the shield of faith, and he was afraid to meet the sword of the Spirit, which is the word of God. He had great respect for that sword. He had felt its keen edge far too often. Yet because of the intensity of his fury, and because he knew that Ekpe was now more alert, he set about to plan a subtle but very aggressive attack.

In fact, Ekpe's growing experience and observations made him keenly aware that Satan was trying to destroy his church. Therefore, he often exhorted his people to put on the whole armour of God.[30]

Righteousness makes us love what God loves and what is good for us, so it is a *breastplate* that protects our hearts from desiring sinful ways that are harmful to us. The *gospel* teaches that Jesus was the sacrifice for our sins, so the *gospel* equips our feet to stand against the idea of appeasing the gods of the land through animal sacrifices. *Faith* believes in the true God and trusts Him. Therefore, it shields us from fear of false gods. *Salvation* is provided by God. It is a helmet to protect our heads from thinking we are dependent on the deceased ancestors rather than God.

The *word of God* is truth, so it is a sword to cut down the falsehood that would lead us away from God. Therefore, we need to give attention to God's word, the Bible. Even though we have God's armour on, we should always have a watchful attitude of prayer. Satan is always trying to find an unguarded spot or a weak place in our armour.

In spite of this, Ekpe was not spiritually prepared for what Satan was planning against him. The old Devil knew that if he could trick Pastor Ekpe into some impropriety, it would deal the young tender church a death blow. His strategy to accomplish this was very crafty, and it was as evil as it was nasty. The driving force of his plan would again be fear.

Satan knew Boma had drifted from God and had laid his armour off. He was the kind of person who would be easy

---

[30]Ephesians 6:14-18

prey. Therefore, he began his plot to get Pastor Ekpe by whispering angry impatient thoughts to Boma. *Why was Ekpe taking so long to come up with the money for Ebitimi. If he were really a man of God, he would have enough faith to lay hold of the dowry immediately.* The more Boma thought the angrier he became. Finally he resolved to corner Ekpe and give him an ultimatum. He would have exactly six weeks to come up with the full amount or he could forever forget marrying his daughter.

Boma was so agitated he went straight to his car and started out to find Ekpe. To make his plan more effective, Satan delayed Boma by causing his vehicle to malfunction on the way. This put him at Ekpe's house at the end of the day — a day when Ekpe had worked extra hard and was exhausted. This would guarantee that Ekpe would be at his weakest.

The car roared up to Ekpe's house in a cloud of dust and out jumped Boma. In just five long steps he was at the door knocking loudly. Ekpe had just dozed off in his chair, so the knock brought him straight to his feet with a start. Where was he? What was going on? Sleep had him confused. Then his wits came to him just enough to realize that someone was knocking on his door with intensity. Someone must be in serious trouble. He charged forward, grabbed the latch, and threw the door open. It was a swift move, but Boma was just as swift to enter. Obviously he was very upset.

As Boma unloaded his wrath on Ekpe, Ekpe's heart began to feel heavier and heavier. He was taken completely off guard. He was not spiritually prepared for this onslaught.

Satan's crafty plan was working so far. On and on Boma
berated him. Ekpe was totally confused. He had never seen
Boma act this way before. The fear of losing Ebitimi again
griped his heart and locked his lips. Finally Boma shouted,
"Well, if you cannot say anything to assure me that you really
want Ebitimi and will pay in a short time, then I may not even
wait six weeks! Another man has approached me about her
and has the money in hand."

This latter statement was a total lie. It came directly from
Satan, but making such a threat fitted Boma's furious state of
mind. When Satan inserted the thought in his mind, he blurted
it out. Then he left in a huff while Ekpe was still trying to get
his thoughts to form into words. Only as Ekpe heard the
motor start did the full implication of the situation hit him. He
ran out the door screaming for Boma to wait, but Boma was
in such a wrought up state of mind that he would not listen.
He stomped the accelerator to the floor and sped away even
faster than he had come.

But this was just the beginning of Satan's nasty, sinister
plot. Nkese's family had not forgotten the humiliation of
Ekpe's refusal to marry her. Her brother Asuquo was especially bitter. He had seen Boma's car go by his place and had
observed it stopping in front of Ekpe's house. He had also
seen Boma angrily charge out of his car to pound on Ekpe's
door. Guessing that things might not be going well between
Boma and Pastor Ekpe, he was waiting for Boma's return.
When he saw the car coming back, he ran to the road and
waved for Boma to a stop. Then Asuquo demanded, "Why
have you come to our village so abruptly, and why are you

leaving in such haste at this time of night?"

Boma didn't answer him directly. He really didn't want to report his private business to an obvious enemy of the faith, but because of his reckless attitude he spouted, "If Pastor Ekpe cannot find the money for my daughter, he might have to settle for your sister yet." Then he shouted, "Excuse me, please," and sped away.

The turmoil of Ekpe's mind after his rude awakening kept him awake most of the night. But finally toward dawn he was able to get a degree of peace by committing the matter to the Lord as much as his tired mind would let him. Therefore, he was sleeping soundly and later than usual when again there was a knock on his door. The first knock did not awaken him. It only triggered a dream of Boma knocking on his door to tell him he was betrothing Ebitimi to another man.

Beside himself, and still asleep, he charged to the door and grabbed the man he thought was Boma and shook him violently. Then suddenly he awakened with Asuquo's angry contorted face staring at him. Immediately, Ekpe released his grip.

"Sorry!" he pleaded, "I was dreaming. Please forgive me."

"Oh why is the gentle pastor of the holy church so agitated this morning?" sneered Asuquo.

"Sorry! Please, I am sorry! I tell you I was having a nightmare! Come in. You are welcome."

Stepping in, Asuquo said, "If you would stay away from that gin at night you would not be sleeping so late. I think your flock will be interested to know that their highly esteemed pastor is giving himself to ufofop."

"Surely you wouldn't report such a story. Do you see any evidence of ufofop in this place?"

"We will leave that for now. In fact we shall forget it altogether, if you will cooperate with me. Really I believe you will see that you do not have much choice anyway. You see, Boma stopped by to see me last night. He said that the betrothal of his daughter to you was all off because there was no way that he would allow his daughter to ah . . ." Asuquo paused for only a moment because Satan interjected a lying thought into his mind. Then he began again, "Well ah . . . ah . . . ." He paused again for the thought to fully develop in his mind. "Boma said there was no way that he was going to let his daughter marry a drunkard."

"No, that cannot be true. I exhort you to be truthful."

"Well, you see the evidence is against you. Many in the village saw Boma drive here in a fury and stop abruptly at your door. They also saw him charge to your door in anger. You will not be able to convince them that he did not come because he heard you were giving yourself to ufofop and then caught you in the very act. They will believe this if I drop the news in their ears," Nkese's brother suggested with a devilish grin. Then he paused long enough to let the implication settle into Ekpe's mind.

"You would not do such a thing!"

"Well you see, if you should see fit to follow your obligation to marry my sister as was arranged when you were a baby, I would forget the whole matter." Ekpe was dumbstruck, but Asuquo continued, "I shall give you some time to think about the matter. In the meantime I shall drop the news into a couple of ears to help you know that I am serious." Then he left as Ekpe stared after him.

Asuquo took stock of what he had said after he left Ekpe's house. He really hadn't intended to threaten Ekpe with the lie, but the idea just popped into his head. He was actually amazed that he was able to think rapidly enough to compose the story as he was telling it. Of course, he did not know that the whole thought process had come from Satan. Asuquo was not sure he would carry out his threat. It would probably be too risky. Such a lie could backfire on him. On the other hand, if the threat brought Ekpe around to his wishes, his purposes would be served.

CHAPTER THIRTEEN

Emeka had become known as a powerful evangelist. His sermons on repentance drove conviction to hearts, and his portrayal of Jesus dying in our place brought people sobbing to the altar. Though he had enjoyed a great measure of success, he kept himself reminded of His dependency on God. As a result, he had become very sensitive to the voice of God's Spirit.

Thursday morning found him in his room studying for the series of sermons he was scheduled to preach the following week. In his meditation, suddenly he envisioned Ekpe laying crushed to the ground under a mammoth rock. Every time Ekpe took a breath, the rock would push him deeper into the earth. Some sneering men stood nearby watching, and their leader kept hollering to Ekpe, "Agree to our terms and we will save you."

Instantly Emeka knew Ekpe needed his help. He would go and find him regardless of how long it took. Twenty minutes later he was out to the road, dressed in fresh clothes, flagging down a taxi.

Four hours later he arrived at Ekpe's village. As the taxi headed toward Ekpe's house, Emeka saw Ekpe approaching on his motorcycle. Emeka quickly rolled the window down and excitedly waved at his friend as he bid the driver to stop. Immediately, Ekpe applied the breaks to his cycle and came to a screeching halt. Emeka opened the door of the taxi and jumped out. "What a surprise!" exclaimed Ekpe, "Welcome, Welcome, Welcome. What brings you here?"

"Can I not come to see my friend without a specific reason?"

"Sure! The fact is, I suddenly realize that I am in great need of talking to you. Maybe God has sent you. No, not maybe, I know God has sent you. I was just on my way out of the village. You caught me just in time. Pay the driver, and we will go to my house where we can talk."

"As the driver turned and drove away, Ekpe stared after the taxi as though in a trance. Then suddenly he turned his cycle around and said to Emeka, "Climb on."

Minutes later they entered the house. "Have a seat, brother," commanded Ekpe. "I will hide my satchel and then be with you." When he returned, Ekpe dropped to his chair and said, "Welcome."

"Thank you for the welcome. How is your family?"

"They are blessed."

"And what about you?"

"We will soon discuss that. How are things going for you and your family?"

"Very well. We are blessed."

With the traditional greetings exchanged, Ekpe demanded with desperate, piercing eyes, "What is the real reason you came? Did you know I needed you?"

"I saw you in my room four hours ago."

"What? You saw me in your room four hours ago? No I was at the bank four hours ago, and I...I...I drew some money out. In fact, yes! Oh yes! You must have seen me. No, you did not really! What did you say? You saw me?" It was obvious that Ekpe was both startled and confused.

"Yes, I saw you under a huge rock."

"That is amazing. Evidently, God was showing you that I was about to be crushed. Tell me more! Just what all did you see!"

"I saw you pressed to the ground under a huge rock. You couldn't throw the rock off, and it was pushing you deeper and deeper into the earth. Men stood by demanding that you agree to their terms. You would not accept their terms, so they refused to help you. I was very alarmed. I felt a great urgency to come to you."

"How thoughtful of you, my brother! You are truly my brother in the Lord, though you are not of my kin. My own kin do not care as much as you do. But I believe I have discovered how to remove the crushing weight."

Ekpe went on to explain the demands of Boma and Asuquo. He described his fear and his desperation to save Ebitimi for himself. He trembled and wept as he poured his heart out. "I have been beside myself with fear and anxiety. I knew I had to do something. But now that you have come. Now that my head is begining to clear—oh no, what have I done? Well, I have not done it yet. It is not too late."

"Ekpe, what are you saying? I now sense that awful fear that I sensed when I saw you in my room. What were you about to do?"

"Emeka, it was terrible. I was under such pressure that I was not thinking correctly. As you saw me, I was about to be crushed. I saw no other way out. I am ashamed to tell you, but I drew money out of the bank that was there for building our new church. I guess I was thinking I would borrow it. I guess I was thinking I would repay it in time to build the church. I cannot honestly say what I was thinking for sure, but I was going to use the money to pay the dowry for Ebitimi."

Ekpe sobbed more; he sobbed loudly. Emeka's heart went out to him. Finally when Ekpe had composed himself, he said, "I must return the money. It would be wrong to use it for the dowry. I don't have any idea how I would repay the money. Besides, it is not right to use the money that has been intrusted to me for building the church in this way. God has sent you Emeka to bring me to my senses."

"I have done nothing, Ekpe. You have seen the error of your ways without a word of condemnation from me."

"*Oh, but the person who eats eggs should not forget the pains suffered by the hen that lays them.* You have put forth great effort to be here for me. When I saw you, I suddenly remembered that I needed to be accountable to people and God. Furthermore, you provided a safe confidential ear in which to unload my emotions. As I unloaded, I saw what I was doing. Oh now I understand why people go astray and eventually become corrupt.

"By God's help, I will always stand against dishonest gain, but I will also have a heart for those who have gone astray as I show them a better way. I am so glad you have come, Emeka. I shall always be indebted to you." Again Ekpe broke into sobs.

"Let us pray," requested Emeka.

"Yes, indeed!"

"Father in heaven, help my brother Ekpe. You know he has erred. You know he has sinned. He sinned first by getting his eyes off of your power to help him and lowering the shield of faith. He sinned second by trusting his poor human ways. Then he sinned by greedily following the devil's wicked suggestion that came to his clouded mind. Yet you know that Ekpe did not want to do wrong. His heart is after you. Therefore, forgive him, and restore comfort and healing to his heart. You know the strain he has been under."

Emeka prayed on, and Ekpe prayed with him. They prayed until they both felt heaven come down, and it seemed that the angels surrounded them. When they finally quit praying there was a confidence that God had the situation in hand.

The Holy Spirit was saying, "As you trust Me I take charge of the situation."

Suddenly Ekpe went for the satchel and returned saying, "Please go with me."

Together they rode the motorcycle into the city, and together they entered the bank. As they entered, they heard a man talking loudly to the bank officer. "Did you not see the note that specified that no money was to leave this account without a written request declaring what portion of the Church building the money was to be used for?"

The friends looked at each other. Their faces that had been serene with confidence suddenly showed alarm as they turned to flee.

CHAPTER FOURTEEN

Just as Ekpe and Emeka turned to flee out of the bank, Ekpe suddenly stopped and grabbed Emeka's shoulder. "I cannot do this. I cannot let fear dictate to me again. I must go and face what happens. I will trust God."

Quickly he stepped up to the counter and said to the cashier, "I want to deposit money in the Eniong Effiom Church account."

As he did this, he saw the man who was talking about the church account. He was talking with the bank supervisor. It was Okokon, one of the three businessmen that had given the money for the church building. At the same moment Ekpe saw Okokon, Okokon saw him. Their eyes locked on each other.

Okokon listened as Ekpe proceeded with his transaction. Okokon heard the cashier say, "That brings your account back to the balance that was there this morning before you drew the money out."

"That is correct," replied Ekpe. Then he said, "I also think that Okokon—the man back there who has been talking to the supervisor—I think he wants to talk with me."

"Yes, Yes, indeed." responded Okokon.

"I need to talk with you outside," said Ekpe.

"I will get back to you, supervisor," said Okokon as he turned to follow Ekpe. "I need to get an explanation from Ekpe."

The two marched quickly outside to where Emeka was waiting with fear still written on his face. There Ekpe began to relay to Okokon all that had transpired. He confessed all. Then Emeka told Okokon of the crises that had come to Ekpe and the pressure he had been under. He also told of how God had let him see that Ekpe was in trouble and needed help.

Okokon began to see that Ekpe was truly contrite. Gradually, the hard, tense lines of his face began to soften. Finally he said, "God bless you, Pastor Ekpe. I understand the pressure you were under. That did not give you the right to withdraw the money, but God has been merciful to you. He knew you were facing a temptation that was more than you could bare. As I heard you preach. 'God *is* faithful and will not allow you to be tempted beyond what you are able, but with the temptation will also make the way of escape, that you may be able to bear it.' [31] God used Emeka to help you find that way of escape. I hold nothing against you."

"How grateful I am to you, Okokon. You have every right to never trust me again, but God has given you a merciful heart. However, under the circumstances I suggest that we set up the building fund account so you have to sign with me for money to be drawn out. This way you will be assured that the money will be used properly, and I will never be tempted again. Please understand that I have learned my lesson, but this arrangement would ensure that I remain accountable. We all are weak, and we all need accountability."

"Pastor Ekpe, I agree with you. We should never have set

---

[31] 1Co 10:13

you up for this kind of a temptation, even though we trusted you fully. I want you to go back with me into the bank to make the change you have suggested. Then I would like to follow you to your house, for I have something else to talk to you about."

*   *   *

"Pastor Ekpe, I have been thinking," Okokon began after he and Emeka had been welcomed into Ekpe's house. "I believe that I can help you with this dowry issue. First I want to take you to see Boma. We will go there in my vehicle. I will try to convince him to take much less money. Then we will return and talk to your uncle. When we tell him of the threats that Asuquo has made, I judge that he will be willing to forgive you for not marrying Nkese. In which case, he should be interested in helping with the dowry for Ebitimi. Finally, I will talk to my business friends about paying what balance remains. We cannot allow God's work to be victimized by those who oppose it."

"Okokon, you are a breath of fresh air!" cried Ekpe. "I am grateful for your initiative and wisdom. Certainly God will bless your efforts."

"Be ready in the morning," replied Okokon as he left for the night.

*   *   *

After the long journey, they neared Boma's house, and Ekpe began to get apprehensive. Would Boma still be angry? Would he even be at home? If they should find him absent, would he be expected to return shortly? Would Ebitimi be there? Would he be able to see her? The tension was mounting. Then he remembered that fear was the tool of Satan. He would not allow fear to defeat him again. He would leave the situation in God's hands. Gradually calmness returned and his faith took hold. God was going before him to prepare the way.

Who should meet them at the door but Ebitimi, as beautiful as ever. Her face glowed at the sight of Ekpe, and his heart took a leap. He could tell that her love for him had not changed.

"Come in," she said. "Have a seat and I will tell Father that you are here."

Lighthearted, she bounced into the other room. Soon Boma appeared. "Welcome," he enthused. "It is good to see you. Sorry about the way I talked to you the other day. Something came over me that I cannot explain."

"Think nothing of it." replied Ekpe. "How are you, and how is your family?"

"We are blessed of the Lord — more than you can know. I will explain soon.

Boma returned the question about family welfare and got assurance that all was well with Ekpe and his kin.

"It is good to see you, Boma. Please meet my friend Okokon. He is a man I highly esteem."

"Welcome, Okokon. I am glad to know that you have good friends like my future son-in-law. I do highly regard him, though I have been rather hard on him."

Ekpe could not believe the change in Boma's tone. God had indeed worked a change in Boma.

Boma continued. "I need to tell you something Ekpe. After I exploded at you the other day, I came home realizing that I had lost touch with God. The fact that I became so angry really shook me. I spent all day yesterday talking to God. He has restored me to a close relationship with Him, and I was planning to come to see you today to apologize. By the way, I want to reduce the amount of the dowry to make things easier on you."

Ekpe wanted to jump up and shout. This news was too good.

"You are doing the right thing," interjected Okokon, without any hint that this is what they had come for.

"Thank you, Okokon. Ekpe, would it help you if I reduced the amount to 35,000 Naira?"

Now Ekpe did jump up. He reached out and grabbed Boma's hand and pulled him up from his seat. He gave Boma a big bear hug, and as he did, he saw Ebitimi's beaming face peaking out from around the corner just before she ducked back. Ekpe was the only one that saw her.

It was unheard of in their culture for a father to offer a reduction of the bride price without being asked to do so. Anyone who did not know the love of God would have said Boma was mad. Even most who claimed to be Christians would have thought him foolish. In a culture where barter is the method of trade, a man did not do such a thing.

Ekpe could do nothing but thank his future father-in-law for his generosity over and over. Then after the talking subsided, Boma implored Okokon and Ekpe to stay long enough for a meal to be prepared for them.

What a sumptuous meal it was! Ekpe noticed that Ebitimi prepared most of it. To realize that he was about to acquire such a fine cook only intensified his joy.

As they were leaving, Okokon declared. "We will plan to be back soon. I have solid reason to believe that God is providing what you require. Thank you! Thank you! And thank you again for your unheard-of generosity."

"Why should I offer my daughter to one who does not love God or to one who loves Him less than Ekpe, just to get more money? Ekpe will raise my grandchildren to love God. That is dowry enough. By allowing him to have my daughter, I shall be paid many times over."

"The future is bright!" declared Ekpe. "Today the works of Satan have been destroyed."

CHAPTER FIFTEEN

Part of Satan's works had been destroyed, but he was not ready to give up the fight. His defeats only served to make him more cunning and ferocious than ever. He was determined to avenge the loss of Boma's cooperation.

Ekpe's heart was light and cheerful. The Wednesday night prayer meeting started with gusto. Prayer rose to heaven from enthusiastic hearts, and faith took hold of the throne of God. Great joy of the Lord flooded the hearts of the people, and this in turn inspired them to pray even more fervently. After an hour, the prayer began to subside, and gradually voices lowered to whispers, as the boundless joy settled into a serene peace. Then the voices of the congregation arose in triumphant song as Pastor Ekpe led them in the well known chorus.

There is joy flowing in my heart.

All my prayers have been answered.

What a difference there was in this meeting from the last prayer meeting. The heart of the pastor was now free from anxiety and frustration.

One by one the people rose to tell of how God was assuring their hearts of deliverance from one problem or another. Simple-hearted faith was connecting the people to God in a way not ever experienced before by this congregation. It struck Ekpe as being very significant that deliverance was being realized without anyone calling for special pastoral deliverance prayers. Evidently deliverance was not solely dependent on the prayer of the pastor or another minister. The key was faith. As faith took hold of the promises of God, the assurance of deliverance was felt in the heart of the person who had faith.

The testimonies of the congregation suggested that they believed they had tapped the source of permanent deliverance from their problems. Even Ekpe was inclined to think that he would never have a serious problem again.

God had definitely revealed himself unto His people, but they would have to learn more about His program. God would use a special process of His kingdom called the "trial of faith" to bring them to a more realistic understanding.

When the service finally ended and the last high-spirited person of the congregation had gone, Ekpe began casually making his way to his house with only the moon to light his path. It was then that he noticed the strange light ahead. It was an eery reddish-yellow color, and it flickered slightly. Perhaps he was seeing the dying embers of someone's cooking fire. But suddenly a glowing figure appeared beside it, and an owl sounded its dreadful hoot three times in a row.

Ekpe felt a freezing chill grip his spine just as a black object swished in front of his eyes, blocking his view. Terrified, he spun around and charged in the direction he had come from, but then he felt the hard, blunt object crash against his scull, as the light of the moon spun away into darkness.

*   *   *

Ekpe's totally confused mind awakened from uncon-sciousness. He saw a slow moving mass of ghosts passing before a dim light. Again terror gripped his mind as he felt his back being pressed against a rough wall by a pressure against his chest. What could be happening? How had his former spiritual exuberance and confidence so suddenly been overcome by this terror? The spirits had gained the upper hand. Where was the deliverance that God had promised?

The level of terror was so high that he was completely disorientated. This fear, combined with the pressure against his chest, caused his breathing to come in short quick gasps. In fact, each succeeding gasp of air became shorter and shorter until his consciousness again faded away.

*   *   *

In this manner, he went in and out of consciousness several times. Finally as he was again cycling back to consciousness, he caught a small hold on faith by remembering the scripture "He shall give His angels charge over you, to keep you in all your ways."[32] This gave him power to grasp the shield of faith. As he took hold of it, he asserted, "The LORD *is* my light and my salvation; Whom shall I fear ? The LORD *is* the strength of my life; of whom shall I be afraid?"[33] Now he was wielding the sword of the Spirit.

Surely God knew about his predicament. A fragment of the assurance he had felt in prayer meeting was being restored. His mind cleared a little more. He cried out, "Jesus help me. Jesus take control of this situation." The pressure on his chest began to ease.

---

[32]Psalm 91:11

[33]Psalms 27:1

Ekpe was still disoriented, but a certain degree of peace returned to his perplexed mind. He realized that what had seemed like a rough wall was really the ground. He was lying on the ground. Then he noticed that what had appeared to be ghosts were really clouds passing by the moon. He was looking straight up at them, because he was lying on his back. This comprehension eased his mind a little more. His exhausted body now drifted into sleep.

It was morning when he awoke. The terror of the night was gone, but the pain he felt caused him to reach for his forehead. There was a wound there. Removing his hand and looking at it, he saw a small amount of blood. So this was not a dream or his imagination. Something had hit him. The startling thought made him spring up to a sitting position. He looked around but nobody was in sight.

Getting to his feet, he gingerly made his way home while keeping a sharp eye on his surroundings. Nothing seemed to be amiss. He arrived at his house and went to the mirror to examine the wound on his head. It was not serious, but a few very small pieces of tree bark clung to the skin. Perhaps he had run into a tree. This thought could explain one part of the horrible nightly episode, but he was sure the rest had been a direct demonic attack.

As he went to pray, the Spirit of God reminded him that even though the attack had been severe, he had gained the victory through faith and his use of the word of God. Faith had been his shield; the word of God had been his sword to drive Satan back. Gradually, his courage mounted and the joy of the Lord returned to his heart. Then God anointed him with boldness, and he resolved that he would go back to the place of last night's attack. He would walk the same path so that he could be assured that God would enable him to stand against any attack that might come without giving way to fear. He would do it that very night.

* * *

Night had come. Ekpe was at the meeting house. His watch showed 9:30, the same time he had left to go home the preceding night. He stepped out of the door. The moon was again shining. Everything seemed the same. He felt the sweat break out on his skin, but he forced one foot forward and then the other.

Step after step, he neared the place of the attack. Then suddenly, the same ghost-like thing appeared, and with it came the same grip of fear on his spine. But the ghost disappeared with the next step. He wanted to run, but he stopped. He held steady. Fear coursed down his spine. He was afraid to step back, but by the shear force of his will, he forced his foot back. Yes indeed! There was the ghost again. It stayed as long as he held this position, but when he stepped back, or when he stepped forward, the ghost disappeared. He also noticed someone looking out of the lighted window of a house some distance away.

Ekpe thought of Peter walking on the water and how he had failed to keep his eyes on Jesus. He would not make that mistake. He forced his mind to think of God. It seemed he could see the face of Jesus saying, "Hold steady." Fear began to subside. He was now ready to walk further down the path. But then he thought of the thing that had swished in front of his face. Just as he did he heard it again, but this time it hit him on the head. The startling effect was like a electrical charge shooting through his body. A wave of fear rushed over him. He could barely control his thoughts to hang on to faith — to trust in God.

Another wave of fear swept over him, but he held steady. Wave after wave followed. Satan was determined to overwhelm him. Yet Ekpe's grip on faith was getting stronger, but then the swishing thing hit him again across his face and against his nose. He felt its sharp edge, like the edge of a knife. His heart was pulsating rapidly. He wanted to run, but he willed his legs not to move. Cautiously, he looked up out of the corner of his eye. The branch of the short palm tree was gently swinging in the breeze. Eh-henh! So that was it. He breathed a deep sigh of relief.

Maybe there had been no attack from the spirit-world after all. Eh-henh! But there had been! Yet the attack had been primarily fear. The demons had inserted fear into natural events. Perhaps they had also been able to manipulate the natural events, but God was the supernatural force on which he would depend. Strength began to seep back into Ekpe's body, but then he remembered the ghostly appearance. How could that be explained naturally? And what about the reddish-yellow flicker that appeared just before he saw the ghost? In the morning he would investigate.

*　　*　　*

Early morning found Ekpe back on the path, walking to the building that seemed to be reflecting light. Eh-henh! There it was. On the very corner of the building was a long piece of bright, new, zinc metal. Normally, one only nailed corrugated zinc metal sheets to the roof, but there it was positioned vertically on the corner of the house. It was probably there to cover a crack in the wall. The length of the zinc was about the same length as the ghostly appearance he had seen the night before. This zinc must have reflected the light shining from the window of the house some distance away. The angle of the corrugation had made the reflection visible only from a certain position. This was why he could see the reflection from only one place on the path.

As he thought about it, it also became quite obvious to him that somebody's outside cooking fire had reflected on the zinc. This caused the reddish-yellow flicker of light that first scared him.

A few things remained unexplained such as the pressure on his chest that pressed his back to the ground, but Ekpe was now ready to admit to himself that the main cause of his scare was fear itself. He felt kind of foolish, but he also felt a great satisfaction in knowing that he was beginning to learn how to overcome fear. He was learning to hold the shield of faith against Satan's the darts of fear and wield the sword of the Spirit which is the word of God.

Ekpe was beginning to understand that many issues of life fall apart when one fails to hold faith against fear. He could also see that when one succeeds in holding faith against fear, things begin to come together.

CHAPTER SIXTEEN

Because Ekpe was learning to trust God in the face of fear, he could now help members of his church when God allowed them to go through the trial of faith. He spent much time counseling and encouraging, and as he did, he continued to gain more insight. His heart was getting braver and more courageous, but the confidence he felt was based in God's power not his own. He knew very well that he had to be vigilant and prayerful at all times.

As relationship between pastor and people developed and the Holy Spirit continued to manifest His presence in the services, the church matured greatly and continued to grow. The building of the new church structure had begun. The Christians were excited.

As before, Ekpe was anxious to get married, but everyone had agreed that the marriage should wait until the new church building was ready. It was a time for developing patience.

Just after breakfast on a Wednesday morning, who should show up at Ekpe's door but Musa. Ekpe was overjoyed. He often thought of Musa and was hoping to go visit him when things slowed down.

Of course Musa asked about Ekpe's welfare and that of his family. He was thrilled to learn that Ekpe's mother had turned to the Lord. When Ekpe asked about his welfare, Musa began a very interesting account of how God was working in his community as he was learning to trust God.

"As you know, I tend to be quite radical. With me it was

all or nothing when I started trying to minister to my people in the north. Of course my Muslim clan is just as radical. They were vehemently opposed to me preaching that Mohammad was a false prophet. In fact, on one occasion I discovered there was a plot to kill me. Only by the mercy of God was I delivered.

"But through that experience I learned some valuable lessons. Since then I have been careful not to compromise any truth. I am still determined that I will not allow any falsehood to be mixed with God's truth."

"Amen!" interjected Ekpe.

"Yet I learned to use another approach. I go out of my way to show love to my people. Many have been amazed that I have purposely shown kindness to my enemies — even those who wanted to kill me. This approach is going a long way. A few of my clan have even started to attend our services. In these services I also stress the love of God and that this love sent Jesus to the cross. It is more difficult for the Muslim leaders to stir up anger at the Christians when all that the people see from us is love.

"Another good thing is happening. In any community there are a lot of people who are indifferent to the passionate concerns of any religion. At least sixty percent of the people in my part of the country are this way. Increasingly, these people are developing great interest in the gospel, even though only a few are attending our services at this time. However, enough awakening is happening to convince us that God is beginning to work a great change in our community."

"Can you give me an example?" asked Ekpe.

"Yes, I can. Yakubu lives about a ten minute walk from our place of meeting. He was in the habit of walking by our place of meeting every day. Quite often he would go by while we were having services. Sometimes we would be singing praises to God. Sometimes we would be praying, and at other times I would be preaching.

"Yakubu was a nominal Muslim, and sometimes he would respond to the daily call to pray, etc. But when he heard us pray with enthusiasm and joy, he was very impressed. The singing also attracted him. He later testified that he learned most of our songs from just walking by while we were singing. He would sing them to himself when he was alone. He thought that he would receive the joy we expressed while singing. But the more he sang our songs the worse he felt because they would remind him of his sins.

"He longed for the joy we had. Then one day he was going by while I was preaching. He suddenly stopped as I declared that God's way was the way of serving others and that it was quite the opposite from self-centeredness.

"This thought blew his mind. He had become convinced that all religions were designed to make others serve the interests of the ones who were promoting them. Yakubu stood on the path and listened for a long time and then went on his way. I saw him that day and was praying for him in my spirit as I preached.

"About three weeks later, he came straight to the meeting house and sat down to enjoy the service. God's presence was being felt in a special way. Deep conviction settled down upon him, and at the end of the service he responded to my call to come forward and pray to be born again. He got soundly converted that morning and has since really been on fire for God. He has led at least eleven people to Christ, and has influenced scores of others to be sympathetic toward us. Some of those are people who have not yet been converted but are attending the services."

"That is a great report!" responded Ekpe. "Can you stay and tell my congregation about this tonight in prayer meeting?"

"I would be glad to do so."

"Real good!

* * *

That night the Holy Spirit again manifested His presence in the praying, singing, and testifying. There was such a serene sense of God that it seemed one could just reach out and touch Him.

In this atmosphere, Musa rose to report the victories in the north. From the very first, people hung on to every word. As he told about Yakubu getting saved and about the awakening in the community, the people became alive with exuberance and joy. There were shouts of "Praise the Lord!" and "Hallelujah!" all over the place. After Musa sat down, the people stood up as one with hands raised to heaven praising the Lord.

Ekpe noted that God did not always manifest Himself in the same way. Sometimes He was felt as a calm sweet presence that brought a serene peace to His people. At other times God electrified the people so that they expressed their joy with boisterous exuberance. He also noted from the testimonies at the beginning of the service that the people were learning to trust God through adversities. They were beginning to understand that at times it was God's will to allow difficulties (trials of faith) to come. As the trials came, they could build their spiritual fortitude through exercising faith and then seeing how God brought victory though faith.

Sometimes the victory of deliverance came through God's help in building stamina and endurance for the difficulty. At other times, God removed the difficulty. God was in the business of producing strong soldiers for His kingdom. Only as strong soldiers, could they hope to realize their great potential through complete faith and dependency on God.

The service was just about to end when to the great surprise of Ekpe and Musa, in walked Adeyemi. Instantly Musa ran to him and the two embraced with excitement and great joy. "How glad I am to see you!" Musa pronounced with great conviction.

"I am even more glad to see you!" declared Adeyemi.

Ekpe was overjoyed to see these two former rivals in such passionate agreement. He knew that Musa had apologized to Adeyemi after that fight back in Bible College. But he also knew that things had never been quite right between them after that for as long as they were in school together. God was doing great things in the land. Ekpe also greeted Adeyemi with hearty enthusiasm, and soon the three friends were walking down the path toward Ekpe's house.

When they got to the place where Ekpe had been attacked, Ekpe relayed to them all the details of what had transpired. He pointed out the spot on the path where he had seen the reflection of light, the branch that had swished down in front of him, and the tree branch he had run into. Adeyemi and Musa couldn't help being amused. They slapped their hands together and laughed heartily.

After they settled into Ekpe's house for the night, it was time for Adeyemi's account of how God was shaking his home community.

CHAPTER SEVENTEEN

Adeyemi began telling his story.

"As you know, I was entertaining the idea that a chief should not be expected to leave his chieftaincy if he became a Christian, even though being a chief required him to perform fetish rites. Well, this very issue was one of the first challenges I met after I began preaching in my village.

"When I first returned to my village, only nominal Christians were there and they were small in number. The chief, over whom we argued in Bible College, was one of them. He was a friend and I wanted to defend him. Yet by the time I left Bible College, my heart was full of desire to preach the full gospel of Jesus. So when I began preaching to the small band of professed Christians, I found myself denouncing the sins of idol worship.

"This disturbed the chief, so he came to me privately to discuss the matter. He said that if what I preached was true, he could no longer pour libation to the spirits of the ancestors and offer sacrifice to them. This put me in a corner. The man was telling me that my own sermon had convinced him it was wrong to perform such rites. Also, I did not want to excuse sin, so I told him that evidently he was correct. Yes, I know what you are thinking," Musa laughed. "I admitted I was wrong right then and there.

"Anyhow, the chief was serious. He said that the Spirit of God had convicted him that he could no longer perform as he had been. Therefore, I was faced with the responsibility of telling him how he should handle the matter. Should he leave his chieftaincy, or should he remain chief and tell the people that the rites would no longer be performed in his village? The chief demanded the answer. I was the one who had been trained at Bible College. I should have the answer. He would have had no regard for me if I told him I did not have the answer.

"I said that I felt he should remain chief and refuse to perform the rites. His next question was, 'Do you know what you are saying? There are some young men in this village who would like to have an excuse to get rid of me. They grumble against me quite often as it is. If I try to break with tradition, they will raise an uproar and ask for a vote of no confidence.'

"This really put the pressure on me because I felt that whatever happened to the chief would be my responsibility. Here I was. I had debated and studied about this all through Bible College. Now when I was faced with the responsibility of giving God's answer to the problem, I didn't have it. So, I said, 'Let me pray about this and get back with you.' He looked at me like he was disappointed—like I should know the answer off the top of my head. Just like that the Spirit of God said to me, 'Pray right here.'

"'Better yet,' said I, 'Why don't you and I pray about it right here?' 'Sure,' he said.

"I prayed, and after I prayed for a while, he began to pray also. We prayed for about ten minutes. The Spirit of God impressed both of us quite clearly that the chief should remain chief and take his stand. Therefore, the chief called all of the council together. He told them that he was no longer going to perform the rites of ancestral worship.

"If any one of them wanted to pour libation for his family he could, but the chief would not do so for the public meetings. Furthermore, he made it clear that he had no fear of Ogun, the god of iron, or Shango, the god of thunder. The chief read from Jeremiah 10 in the Bible that commands us to not be afraid of these kinds of gods because they do not have power to do good or evil."

"Wonderful!" exclaimed Musa.

Adeyemi continued, "Most of the council sat there stunned. This was such a great surprise to them that they didn't seem to know whether to be alarmed or just angry. Amazingly, they did not resist. They filed out without saying yea or nay. When the chief told me what happened, I also was stunned. Their silence seemed to indicate they were brooding. Perhaps it was the ominous silence that comes before the storm.

"The word spread rapidly, and the chief expected the young men who had opposed him on other issues to really become upset. The way they responded was the real surprise. These young men wanted change, and they were encouraged to see the old chief take a stand on something. They started defending the chief against the criticism of the older men. In the end, there was wide acceptance of the chief's decision. Those who opposed could not rally enough people to their side to make a significant impact."

"It is obvious that God went before you," said Ekpe.

"That is true," agreed Musa, "This shows that God will help every chief, who becomes a Christian, to retain his position, when he becomes willing to take a stand."

"Let me disagree with you on that?" interjected Ekpe. "I have learned not to measure everything by one experience. Remember Shadrach, Meshach, and Abednego?"

"Yes, of course."

"They told the king that God was able to deliver them, but they also said that they did not know if God would deliver them from the fiery furnace. Yet they boldly told the king that they would not bow down to the golden image under any circumstances. What we need to observe from their example is that they made the decision to do the right thing and left the result up to God. We cannot guarantee God will always enable a chief to retain his chieftaincy when he takes a stand for the right way.

"To make another point, I believe Adeyemi did the right thing by engaging the chief in prayer so the chief could get direction directly from God. This also showed the chief his pastor was supporting him as he made the right decision."

"You are very wise, Ekpe" agreed Adeyemi, "I now understand why the Spirit of God directed me to pray with the chief. And now that I think about it, my chief said he was willing to accept what God allowed before he went before the council to proclaim his stand for God. I did not see the significance of that submission to God's will until now."

"Does this mean that God only wants a chief to be willing, so that after he is willing to be removed from his chieftaincy, God will surely protect his position?"asked Musa.

Ekpe replied, "We can never be sure of that. God's ways are higher than our ways. At times He may see that it is best for the chief to accept a demand that he step down from being chief. Submission to God's will is the first step toward receiving help from God. When we finally submit to God's will, we receive pure faith from God—the faith to trust God. Then as we trust Him, He does what is best for us and His kingdom."

"I think I see the light," declared Musa. "I now understand my recent experience of learning to deal with the fear of being murdered for my faith in the north. When I became willing to accept martyrdom at the hands of those who were plotting my death, I received a great peace from God. But the interesting thing was that when I received this peace, I began to have faith that God would deliver me."

"I did not know about this experience of yours until now," responded Adeyemi.

"Ekpe knows," laughed Musa, "I have shared the story of what God is doing in the north with him. You will hear later."

"Okay, but I have heard enough to get your point," declared Adeyemi. "And I experienced that same kind of peace when I was forced to accept the chief's decision that it was wrong for him to perform fetish rites. I wanted to hang on to my argument that it was all right for him to do fetish things, partly because I was still determined to win the argument with Musa. However, when I accepted that I was wrong, my last resistance to God's will was gone. It was then that I experienced the peace you are talking about. Almost immediately after that, I received faith to believe that God would protect the chief's position. If it had not been God's will to protect the chief's position, I would have received the faith to believe and trust otherwise."

"Exactly!" declared Musa. "The light is still coming my way. I am gaining more understanding."

CHAPTER EIGHTEEN

The builders had been working for many months, but now the completed church building stood as a monument to the great spiritual awakening that was taking place in Ekpe's village. What a great day of celebration the dedication had been! And since then the congregation had continued to grow, People were repenting. They were turning from their old sinful ways and turning to God. Their lives told the difference.

Pastor Ekpe had been ordained in the new church, so he was now addressed as Rev. Ekpe. The wedding date of his marriage to Ebitimi was set. Ekpe reflected that God had brought many things together in his life and the lives of many of his friends and associates. Yet he knew that many challenges lay ahead. Dishonesty and corruption of all kinds still prevailed in the land. The resulting dysfunctional patterns were evident everywhere. A great spiritual awakening was needed.

It was in this frame of mind that he felt led to put a trusted elder in charge of his Sunday service and go visit the old church in the heart of the city. It was known to almost everyone within 30 kilometers of its setting.

The church stood in the city, a considerable distance from the market. It was considered orthodox and had been brought here by the colonial pioneer missionaries. The locals had taken it up at the exit of the pioneers missionaries, and it was generally assumed that its doctrines had been maintained. The building was a gigantic edifice made with ancient bricks. It towered to the skies in the sprawling magnificence of a colonial masterpiece and stood as a symbol of religious legacy.

People called it the chapel. They worshiped there every Sunday. It was usually filled beyond its capacity. No other church building had as much significance in the whole district, and it was undoubtedly the most popular.

The hymn flowed from the organ and the mouths of the huge congregation. Gradually, the intensity grew until it could be heard great distances away. Euphoria filled the church. Now, everyone was in high spirits. They sang heartily. It was a familiar hymn, known since long, long ago.

> Rock of ages, cleft for me,
> Let me hide myself in thee.
> Let the waters and the blood,
> From thy wounded side which flowed,
> Be of sin the double cure,
> Save from wrath, and make me pure.

The pastor, an elderly gentleman, rose to preach. He read his scripture, the ten commandments. "Thou shalt not!" he thundered as one by one he expounded with eloquence on all ten. The amens resounded from the congregation — many from sincere hearts. Many other amens came from those who took advantage of the opportunity to profess even though they did not believe. After all, the important thing was not what you were, but what people thought you were. These pretenders seemed totally oblivious to the fact that the omniscient God knew what they really were.

After the service, a group of men rallied around one who was proposing that a committee be formed to establish rules of conduct to combat the moral degeneracy and corruption, in their society. Some of those present declared their agreement. The louder and longer they denounced the corruption upon the land, the more ethical and moral they felt. The very act of becoming indignant at others' evil actions made their own evil hearts seem good, not to mention, that it was good politics.

Ekpe appreciated the sermon and saw value in establishing a standard of conduct from the Bible as applied to the culture. Possibly, it would even be good for a group of godly people to produce a document establishing that kind of a standard. But he longed for the day when the hearts of his countrymen would be changed to love righteousness. He was searching for some solid promise from God's word that he could cling to and recommend as an instrument of spiritual awakening. He wanted something that would bring inner righteousness to the heart, not just the outward legal righteousness of following rules. Ekpe wanted something that would awaken people to the realization that God had power to change people all across the land. In fact, his own heart was hungry for more of God in his own life.

This hunger had increased every time he faced the temptation to give way to fear. Also, the sinful desires that lurked in his heart disturbed him. He keenly felt the conflict between these desires and his love for God. He wanted something that would cleanse his heart of these sinful impulses and give him greater courage in the face of temptation. He had a true hunger and thirst after righteousness and longed to be filled as the beatitude promised.[34]

He stepped outside, hailed the taxi that was approaching, and entered the front passenger seat. The other passengers were taken to their desired destinations, and he was soon left alone with the driver. Realizing Ekpe was a pastor, the driver asked if he wanted to take the rear seat. Ekpe indicated that he was comfortable where he was and declined taking the seat of distinction.

Ekpe was taken up with his thoughts, but the driver wanted to talk. "Reverend, could you tell me what the Bible means by the statement, 'Blessed are the pure in heart for they shall see God?'" The significance of the question stunned Ekpe. The driver was keyed into the very issue that was troubling him, and he was waiting for an answer.

"To have a pure heart is to have a heart that is filled with righteousness, so that one loves what God loves and hates what God hates." Ekpe was amazed at his own answer. He had never articulated this understanding of a pure heart until now. Evidently the raw uncultivated thoughts of his heart had been trying to express this very truth. The direct question from the driver had forced him to put into words what he knew to be true, down deep in his heart, from having studied God's word.

But now the driver was asking another question, "Does that mean that all desire for sin can be removed from one's

---

[34]Matt 5:6

heart?"

The question dug into Ekpe's conscience. "It has to mean that. Otherwise, Jesus would not have said, 'Blessed are they that hunger and thirst after righteousness for they shall be filled.' If we are filled with righteousness, how can any desire for sin remain? Furthermore, Jesus would not have said that the person who has a pure heart shall see God if it had not been possible to have a pure heart." His own answers were convicting his own heart.

"Okay, but what about desires, like the desires for food and clothing, the desire for financial security and the drive for sex, etc.? These often cause us to sin. Should we expect God to remove them?"

"These kinds of cravings and impulses are not sinful; they help us survive and cause humanity to procreate. But a desire to gratify them in ways that hurt others and pervert God's purpose for them is sinful. If we gratify these cravings and impulses as God intended, God is pleased." Again, Ekpe was amazed at the insight that was coming to his own mind as he sought to explain God's word to the driver.

"Pastor, would you pray for me? I have a great hunger to have a pure heart. I know I have been born again, but I sense that a part of me often says no to God and His will. I guess most of my heart says yes to God, but part of my heart says no to Him. I want God to give me a pure heart, so that I will desire His will with my whole heart."

Ekpe was getting backed into a corner. How could he pray for this man to receive a pure heart when he felt the same need. "I will be praying for you as I go," he replied.

"Well, you see I wanted you to pray for me right now as we are going down the road. I can drive and watch the road while you pray."

Now fully backed into a corner, Ekpe began to pray for the man. Amazingly, the Spirit gave him great anointing to pray, but before long he was praying "God give us—the driver and I—pure hearts. We both have the same need. We want to love what You love. We want to hate what You hate."

"Amen!" shouted the driver. "Our hearts need to be changed."

As Ekpe continued to pray, the Holy Spirit brought scripture to his rememberance. "Lord You prayed in John 17 for Your disciples to be sanctified. Our hearts need to be sanctified, set apart to You. Then our hearts will be cleansed of all desire for sin."

*   *   *

The driver joined in the prayer with as much intensity as Ekpe. This alerted Ekpe to the danger of the driver not minding his driving. He was distracted just long enough to discover that the driver had pulled off of the road and stopped. They both continued to pray until their faith took hold of God's promise to give them pure hearts. And as their faith took hold, a great inner peace and rest came to them. Their hearts were cleansed and they were filled with the Holy Spirit. They sensed a new spiritual energy. This was the energy they needed for power over sin and temptation and for power to serve God aggressively. God did His work in their hearts.

Ekpe was aware that the promise of seeing God came to

him. He saw God in a new light. He saw God as the One able to change the heart of his countrymen as God changed his own heart. He saw God as the willing giver of the Holy Spirit and inner righteousness. He saw God as a God of power and might who could effect the change needed in the land. He saw God this way because he felt no condemnation from God[35] to blur his spiritual vision. There was complete openness between Ekpe and God. He sensed no degree of rejection from God. Yes, the promise was true, "Blessed are the pure in heart for they shall see God."[36] This was the promise he had been looking for. He had read it many times in the Bible, but this day was the first time he recognized its full significance.

If the people of his country would become pure in their hearts they would see, through the eyes of faith, that God had the power needed to change the land. This cassava of faith would provide the garri of solid hope that was needed — the hope that his people could cling to. The hope that would not disappoint.[37]

---

[35] Romans 8:1

[36]Matt 5:8

[37] Romans 5:5

CHAPTER NINETEEN

Since Ekpe encountered his own personal Pentecost[38] that night in the taxi with the driver, things had been much different. Wherein he had been fearful like Peter in the Bible before Pentecost, he was now bold and courageousj like Peter after Pentecost. Wherein he had been weak in the face of temptation, hc was now strong. His faith had laid hold of real hope, and he now preached with much greater anointing. However, Satan was now more determined then ever to destroy him. The real contest was already in the making.

All of the many details for Ekpe's marriage to Ebitimi had been taken care of. They would have a Christian version of the traditional marriage, and a church wedding afterward. Eno had given of her meager funds all that she could scrape together to help with the expenses. Uncle Ette had given quite a large sum after he was persuaded to accept Ekpe's decision to marry Ebitimi. Ekpe had contributed his small part, and Okokon and his friends had paid the balance. The food and drinks had been purchased, and everything was in readiness for the traditional marriage that very day at Ebitimi's place.

*   *   *

A huge crowd gathered, and off to one side a palm fronds tent was erected on the grounds for the occasion. In the tent were father Boma and other family members of the bride.

Mother Eno, Uncle Ette, Cousin Ubong, and Ette's other

---

[38] Acts 2:1

sons and daughters arrived with Ekpe and approached the tent. As they approached, Okumagra, the family orator and spokesman of the bride, stood. "Welcome travelers" he enthused with a big smile, as though they were strangers. "Come and receive our drink. We are happy to have you as our guests. We have a table reserved for any entourage, such as yours, that should happen by. You shall have that table."

Ekpe's entourage entered the tent and took the seats provided. Glasses of nonalcoholic drinks were served to them. But before anyone drank, Ubong stood. He was the orator who spoke for Ekpe and his family. "This day it is our pleasure to receive your welcome. It is very kind of you to receive strangers such as we. We are overwhelmed by your generosity, and to demonstrate this we now offer drinks to you."

From the cases they brought, they served their own unfermented drinks to Ebitimi's family. All the while, the air was maintained that none of Ebitimi's family knew the reason they came.

After these were served, Ubong stood again and said, "Please, dear people, I would like to inform you that each one of us is a member of one family, and I want to introduce each member." One by one, he introduced all except Ekpe. Then after much ado about the joy they felt in finding the other family gathered together, Ubong came to the purpose of the visit.

"I want you to know that we were passing by your fair village and noticed a very beautiful flower. Our eyes have been dazzled with that flower ever since. We have now come to ask your permission to cut it and plant it in our yard." Ubong took his seat.

Okumagra arose to respond. "Well, you see we have many flowers. Is it a rose, a hibiscus, a hydrangea, or just what flower are you wanting? Of course it could be that you are really speaking of more than a plant with pretty flowers. If you are speaking in metaphors, come to the point. Please be more specific." He took his seat again.

Ubong rose with a very broad smile. "My good people you surely are pulling my legs. I think you know why we have come, but just in case the true reason of our visit is hidden from you, let me explain in plain language.

"One of our young men was walking by your noble village the other day, when who should appear before his eyes, but one of your damsels of rare beauty and charm. He reported this attraction to us with such eloquent speech that we felt compelled to trace his steps. Of course we did not know where those steps would lead, but with pleasure we discovered that they led us to your village. Now we humbly request that you give this fair lady to our young man in marriage."

It was Okumagra's turn. "Eh-henh! Now you are coming to the point, but we have so many young ladies. We don't know whom you are talking about. Also, some have traveled. It could be that the one you want is not here. However, permit us to call the ladies of the house, so you can point her out if she is here." He called out, "Ladies, these good people have come seeking one of our fair ladies. Please go and see if you can find the lady that these people are looking for and fetch her."

The women left and soon returned with a damsel. They said, "We have found one of our eligible young ladies." Then they danced around her. When they finished, Ubong said, "Please accept my thanks for your trouble, but I must inform you that this fine young lady is not the one. Please bring someone else."

Okumagra gave the command, and the ladies responded by going and again returning with another girl. After they finished dancing around her, Ubong said, "You people are being so gracious. Again you have gone to great effort to find the one that we have come for. Please accept our humble thanks for the second time, but I am sorry to have to say this is not the one."

"Well then,"replied Okumagra, "We will be glad to oblige you and bring the only one left, but at the present she is not here. She has gone to Abuja. It will be expensive to bring her so I must request that you give us money for her flight."

The orators negotiated back and forth on the amount to be paid and finally agreed on N1,000. Soon after, Ebitimi was brought, and the ladies danced with great exuberance. Finally when they finished, Okumagra asked Ubong, "Is this the lady you are looking for? If not we cannot help you."

"Yes," shouted Ubong. All the members of Ekpe's family arose and shoutcd, "Yes! Yes! This is the one we have come for!" They sang and danced and clapped their hands. Finally Ebitimi sat down in a chair beside Ekpe and the dancing stopped.

The master of ceremonies arose and called on Ekpe's family to present the marriage acceptance drink. The drink represented the marriage. This unfermented fruit wine was given to Boma. He called Ebitimi and gave it to her, but she returned it to him, whereupon he asked, "Is this drink presented on your behalf?"

"Yes, it is, my father."

"If I drink this wine will it cause me a problem?"

"No, Father. This will bring you great joy. It will not be a problem to you."

The wine was given to Boma who poured it out in a glass and presented it to Ebitimi to drink. She drank a small amount and gave it back to Boma. He drank the remainder.

The emcee cried out, "Put your hands together for this bride." Everyone present clapped vigorously.

The emcee pronounced, "The family of the groom will now present the family of the bride with what her family has required."

Ubong came forward and asserted that all of the requirements have been met. Okumagra nodded his head in agreement, and the emcee pronounced, "The bride's father and mother have been satisfied."

In response, both families stood to dance and clap their hands. They continued for several minutes and then sat down. They were served more drinks.

The man serving as Ekpe's pastor was then called upon to give advice to the wedding couple. He exhorted them for fifteen minutes, and then Ekpe and Ebitimi knelt together. The pastor prayed for them and for God's blessing on their future.

It was then time for feasting. Both families stood. The emcee brought the head lady of the groom's table to the bride's table where she received garri and pumpkin soup. This she served to the groom's family.

Finally, the young ladies of the bride's family went forth to serve food and drink to the crowd of guests. Everyone feasted and had a good time visiting together and congratulating the couple and their families.

For unbelievers, the traditional marriage involved fetish practices, such as offering a white cock to the ancestors and pouring out libation to their spirits. For Ekpe and Ebitimi, no fetish practices were observed. Also, they did not recognize themselves as married in God's sight yet. Only after the church wedding would Ebitimi come to live with Ekpe and be physically united with him.

Yet this ceremony was a milestone. It was the event that required the most preparation and money. This was one more step toward Ekpe and Ebitimi putting their lives together. A man needed a wife to support him emotionally and spiritually, and a woman needed a husband to love and cherish her. As Ekpe thought back over all the stress and strain involved in bringing him and Ebitimi to this point, he had a thought. He wondered if the coming of Christianity would eventually influence his culture to remove some of the heavy requirements for marriage.

CHAPTER TWENTY

Ebitimi could hardly believe that the day of her wedding was finally at hand. At fourteen, the thought of any possible wedding was like a dream. A wedding had seemed a long time in the future, but now as she looked back, it seemed like yesterday. She was also keenly aware that since then she had greatly matured. Her first tingly feelings for Ekpe had developed into a deep love that held him in high regard. He was not only the most charming man she had ever met, he was a tower of strength and a gifted spiritual leader.

The times they spent together since the betrothal (always with others around) naturally were times of building mutual admiration. But at these times, they also discussed their plans for building God's kingdom. This had increased their passion to give themselves fully to God's work.

They had discussed the role that Ebitimi would play in ministering to other women. Together they felt the need to reach out to those women who felt downtrodden and abused. They agreed that these women needed to be taught to mentally and emotionally sense their value in God's sight. As women gained a greater sense of self-worth, they would expect better treatment from their husbands. But a greater sense of self-worth on the part of the wives would also cause their husbands to respect them more. Then if husband and wife would follow Christian counseling concerning proper marriage relationships, mutual respect and love would develop and the marriage would be enhanced. This would greatly help women to live up to their potential in God. Ekpe and Ebitimi saw a great opportunity for Ebitimi to help women in this way.

Ekpe wholeheartedly affirmed that women had great potential to influence society for the good. They could often do what men could not do. Furthermore, Ekpe decried the commonly held belief that women were more susceptible to demon possession and evil than their male counterparts. He recognized that women (as well as men) could be more inclined to mischief if they were made to feel like second-class citizens. But given their rightful place in society, other cultures had shown that godly women often became a greater influence for morality than men. In all of their discussions, Ebitimi had grown to greatly admire Ekpe. No other man had even the slightest chance of distracting her attention from him.

Needless to say, her thoughts of Ekpe were not just in these areas. She was a normal woman and found that her heart was ever warming to him. Often she felt that tingly feeling that had first come to her at fourteen. This would carry her to lofty heights of romantic anticipation and make her twirl and dance about.

Okonkwo, Emeka, Musa, and Adeyemi were all planning to be at the church wedding and to have a part in the ceremony. The plans were simple, yet Ekpe and Ebitimi, along with their families and friends, had prayed much for God's guidance. This was a very important occasion. It would mark a significant change in the village. The significance was that Christianity was replacing the traditional religion. It was challenging the long held institutions of worship that paid homage to the spirit-world. And it was bringing hope where hope was needed.

However, because of Ekpe's guidance, the Christians had been very respectful of those who still held to the old way.

No intentional attack had been made on those who believed in the old worship. No public demonstrations had been staged against fetish practices, and no authority in the hierarchy of the village government had been directly challenged. Yet because the truth of the Bible exposed the falsehood of the old system, many were turning from it.

Satan had lost one battle after another that he had waged against the truth. Where truth was proclaimed, his system of falsehood and fear immediately began losing its grip. When people placed their faith in God, their faith became a shield to protect them against his darts of fear. Therefore, the fear of the gods of the land was eroding. In short, Satan was losing the spiritual war.

Yet, by inspiring Asuquo to spread the lie that Ekpe was giving himself to the locally made gin, Satan had made a little headway. Some of the villagers still looked at him with skeptical eyes, but Satan needed something that would strike deeper—right to the very heart of the church. The former steadily progressing spiritual awakening had recently developed into a full-blown rapidly expanding movement. The main cause of this was the new emphasis on receiving a pure heart and being filled with the Spirit.

Soon after Ekpe had his personal Pentecost, he again met with Emeka the evangelist who also gave testimony to having recently had his heart cleansed of sinful affections and filled with the Spirit. Emeka had been so on fire that Ekpe scheduled him for a series of nightly revival meetings. Emeka's message of holiness was just what the people of Ekpe's congregation were hungry for. As they responded to heart cleansing, they were so filled with God's Spirit that they became virtual human dynamos of spiritual power. They testified everywhere of their love for God and the victory over sin that they were experiencing. Their joy was overflowing, and the resultant holy enthusiasm was spreading like a grass fire in the Harmattan.[39]

Now this victory was going to be accentuated with a very highly advertized Christian wedding in the very church that was responsible for the revival movement. Satan saw that he must immediately do something so drastic and powerful that it would penetrate the physical realm. In this way he could mount a tangible force against those involved in the powerful movement of spiritual awakening. Otherwise the momentum that had developed against evil would forever overwhelm Satan's forces.

Satan already had the heart of Asuquo, the son of Abia Ibok, firmly in his grasp, so he could begin his new offensive there. Yet Satan needed a greater foothold—something that penetrated the natural world. If he could stir up enough bitterness in Asuquo's heart, Asuquo would so fully open himself to evil that he could possess his body. This was hardly a new tactic for Satan. He had done this very same

---

[39]The dusty winds blowing down from the Sahara
Desert in the dry season

thing to Judas two thousand years ago.

Asuquo could not get over the fact that Ekpe had jilted his sister, Nkese, to say nothing of Christianity's assault on his father's practice. In former times, his father made a handsome living because his fetish medicines were greatly in demand. Now he was rarely called upon once a week. The Christian God was so powerful that the medicines seemed very weak by comparison. Furthermore, Christians taught that it was wrong to place faith in his father's potions because they were connected to the worship of the ancestors and the gods of the land.

However, the planned wedding, featuring Ekpe marrying the Christian Ebitimi (instead of Nkese) in the new church gave Asuquo a target on which to vent all of his bitterness. As he contemplated the attack, his bitterness continued to mount until it be came a force powerful enough to push him over the edge. Therefore, in an attitude of exceeding rage, he gave himself over to the desire to craft evil.

This was what Satan was looking for. The door was now wide open. Without delay, he sent many of his demons scrambling to possess Asuquo's entire being. They took possession of his mind, including the motor controls of his muscles. This gave Satan control of his body motions and his speech. Asuquo had become his literal slave, and he would find that his master was a merciless tyrant.

Asuquo had been complaining to the Etubom, the chief of the village, about the wedding, but now he charged to his palace to demand action. Fearing such wrath, the Etubom felt pressured into secretly summoning those of the council who had not yet converted to Christianity. Here Asuquo was permitted to express his grievances. He so successfully communicated bitterness that the council became determined to take immediate action. In their vengeful anger, they poured out libation to the ancestors and called on the gods of the land to arise and fight. Three of the council men became so agitated that Satan could also send his demons into them.

*   *   *

Of all Ekpe's ministerial friends, Adeyemi had the most poise and the greatest ability to articulate with passion. He was the true orator and had great confidence in speaking. He was just the right person to portray the relationship one could have with his maker as exhibited in the institution of earthly marriage.

For more than an hour, Adeyemi held the congregation spellbound with his well-prepared message. His description of the beauty of an intimate relationship with Christ spoke to the spiritual imaginations of those whose spirits were already tuned to God through Ekpe's ministry. Heaven seemed very close and God exceeding powerful. The spiritual ecstasy of the people rose to a crescendo, but then things began to change.

An uninvited man slipped into the foyer and an unsuspecting usher took him to a seat in the rear. A chill began to settle over the congregation. The people who had formerly been enraptured in the message now began to get restless. Soon the room began to darken as the formerly bright sky outside began to get cloudy. Gradually, the clouds got thicker and the room got darker. Those looking out the windows noticed vultures beginning to appear below the clouds.

Suddenly, a loud blast was heard outside and then another. The service was disrupted. Some rushed to the door. Others stood to look out the windows. Men with chalk-covered faces, holding machetes, emerged out of the bushes that stood not far from the church on all sides. The place was surrounded with the fierce-looking masqueraders. Two of them were holding double-barreled shotguns. The women screamed and the children began to cry.

Okonkwo and Musa were in the rear serving as ushers. They immediately appraised the situation and Okonkwo stepped outside before Musa could stop him. A grotesquely masked man approached with his machete held high but then stopped and stared at Okonkwo. Okonkwo noticed that the masked man's manner of walking was that of Asuquo, but he also felt great spiritual strength enter his being. All fear vanished.

Inside, Musa also felt the same kind of holy power infusing his being. A great calmness came over him. He began exhorting the panicking crowd to be quiet, hold steady, and see the salvation of the Lord. Eventually they responded to his words and began to get quiet. They sat down and assumed a watchful attitude, though fear was still written all over their faces. Then they began to pray.

Outside the battle raged. Men were yelling and dancing about. Some hacked the church with their knives. The guns sounded off again and again. One shot penetrated the side of the building and blew a hole through the roof. Then another penetrated lower on the wall. A child screamed but then buried his face in his mother's dress for comfort. A third shot came through a window just above the heads of the people. Then suddenly everything was quiet.

The masked man approached again. Okonkwo stood his ground—his nerves steady—a peace within. Closer and closer came the man who walked like Asuquo. He stopped again, tilting his head to one side and then to the other, all the while keeping his eyes glued to Okonkwo.

Okonkwo took a step forward. The man swung his machete toward him menacingly. Okonkwo took another step forward. The masked man now lifted his knife ready to strike. Okonkwo took another step forward. Several people from inside the church were looking out the door at the contest. All praying stopped. Everything was deathly quiet.

To Okonkwo it seemed the Holy Spirit said, "You must be my martyr. Today you must face off with the enemy. What happens is none of your concern. Others do not have the martyr gift. They have not mastered fear, but you have been endowed with special courage. I am depending on you to demonstrate the courage of unwavering faith right up to the last moment. Then those looking on will also take courage. Stand firm. Your reward is in heaven."

*   *   *

The masked man stepped toward him. He was less than a meter away. He was still holding his machete up for the strike. He slowly lowered it until Okonkwo felt the sharp cutting edge against his neck.

At that moment, Okonkwo saw through the dark overcast

to the throne of God with Jesus standing at the right hand of God. He felt the knife begin to cut into his flesh. Like Steven in the Bible[40] he lifted his hand, pointed to heaven, and cried, "Look!" He was ready to say, "I see Jesus," when suddenly the vision disappeared. He blinked his eyes and saw the masqueraders backing away. The one who had been pressing the knife into his neck fell backward. His machete clattered against the ground.

* * *

Okonkwo was now experiencing a great let-down. He had been full of heavenly joy expecting to go to heaven and be with Jesus and the angels. To him it had seemed that his spirit was already there. He cared not for life on this earth. What a disappointment!

Then he began to comprehend the awesome, inexplicable defeat of the enemy. The chalk-faced men were slinking off in fear, but every now and then they glanced over their shoulders toward the sky. Then as Okonkwo looked in the same direction, he saw that a great hole in the clouds had appeared and was rapidly getting larger and larger. The clouds were disappearing. The vultures were winging higher and higher and further and further away. The sun was shining again. So God had asked him to be a martyr only to spare his life.

He looked down to see the masked man, whom he suspected to be Asuquo, still lying on the ground. He writhed

---

[40]Acts 7:56

and squirmed. "Let me out of here!" he cried, but no one was holding him. He screamed louder, "Let me go from this place!" A power was holding him back. "Please! Please! Let me go from your presence." His gaze was fixed on Okonkwo.

"Go!" commanded Okonkwo. Instantly, the man scrambled to his feet and fled away as fast as his legs could carry him, leaving his machete lying on the ground.

*　　*　　*

Shouts emerged from inside the church.

"Praise the Lord!"

"Hallelujah!"

"Praise the Lord!"

"Hallelujah!"

Some clapped their hands. Others lifted their hands to heaven and offered thanks to the Lord. Never had anyone witnessed such a scene before.

But strangely, all fear was replaced with boldness and a calm peace. The atmosphere seemed to have a scent of freshness. The people of Ekpe's church saw God in a new light. Like Isaiah in the Bible, they had seen Him, high and lifted up.[41]

The wedding could now proceed. It was decided that Adeyemi's sermon received confirmation in the great victory just experienced. Ekpe and his groomsmen, Emeka, Ubong, Okonkwo, and Musa took their places at the altar.

The wedding march began and the bridesmaids marched

---

[41]Isaiah 6:1

one by one down the isle. Finally, Ebitimi came down the isle on her father's arm. Ekpe's heart leapt for joy. She was beautiful beyond description. Adeyemi asked the question, "Who giveth this woman to be married to this man?" Boma answered, "Her mother and I do."

Ekpe's heart cried out, *Yes, she is given to me! Yes, she is given to me!* The rest was all a blur. The solos sung by friends, the prayers, the vows, the marriage kiss, and the admonition until Adeyemi said, "And now I pronounce you husband and wife." Suddenly Ekpe was brought to reality like awakening from a dream as Adeyemi continued, "Ladies and Gentlemen, I present to you Reverand and Mrs. Ekpe Ikpok Eto."

* * *

That night the marriage was consummated as Ekpe and Ebitimi spent their first night alone. Ekpe and Ebitimi had become husband and wife. God had brought them together, and this reality spoke to them that God was putting many other things together in the land.

EPILOGUE

Ekpe's village continued to progress as the truth of God shown more and more light into her darkened corners. Old patterns were broken. Minds were enlightened. The joy of the Lord gave new energy and zest to living. A high level of kindness became the expected etiquette. Mercy was shown to all around, even to those of other tribes, because the barriers of tribalism broke down. Honesty prevailed in business dealings. Ways to work together were discovered.

The unheard of happened. Through the mutual pooling of funds, the village imported technology and equipment to build its own electrical power plant. By cooperating to conserve usage, it became possible to have uninterrupted electrical power during the daily scheduled times. Nowhere else in the land did any community experience such consistency of electrical power.

Then the really astounding thing happened. A team of businessmen came from the United States to explore the possibilities of establishing a factory on the edge of the village. Why? Because word had reached their land through an American missionary that here was a community that could function together in truth and honesty.

The result was that a very profitable manufacturing business was built, and 530 people of the village were employed with adequate monthly wages.

Other marks of a high level of functionality also became apparent. Several men and women from the village formed an organization for helping those injured by accidents (especially traffic accidents) and robbery. They named their organization "Let Me Help Without Blame" (LMHWB). A certificate of membership was prepared for all who should be permitted to join. This is the way it read.

Member Certificate of
Let Me Help Without Blame

Let it be known to all that___(name of member)___wants to be free to help any person who shall be injured by accident or robbery that he/she deems himself/herself capable of aiding, without implication that he/she has caused said injury. We certify that the above named person is a reputable person worthy of helping the injured without blame. Please help us help our society by not blaming this individual for injuring the person he/she could be aiding at this time. We endeavor to show mercy as Jesus taught us by the story of the Good Samaritan in the Bible.

President_____

Vice President_____

Many villagers rallied to become members, and began courageously getting involved. They came upon traffic accidents along the road and stopped to help. They took the seriously injured to the hospital and thus saved lives. Some of the members had to answer for their deeds in court, but when the judge was informed of their organization and its mission they were exonerated.

Of course the hospitals, to which the injured were brought, began demanding payment. The hospital expenses were mounting. However, one hospital administrator was a member of the large City Church that Reverend Ekpe had visited that day the elderly minister preached on the ten commandments. That administrator told his church of LMHWB and the logistic problem they were causing.

The pastor and the elders called the leaders of LMHWB and asked for a meeting with them. In the meeting the big church agreed to join the good Samaritan effort by establishing a monetary fund. They would name the fund "Money For Injured People" (MFIP). Then they launched MFIP by a highly advertized meeting with famous speakers. Thousands came to the meeting, and the idea of becoming a good Samaritan really caught on. A large offering was raised and many pledged to continue supporting the fund with monthly or yearly gifts. The hospital's logistic problem had been met, and many joined LMHWB. Soon other churches got involved as people became convicted that *to receive mercy from God one must show mercy.*[42] The fire was started that would change the whole attitude of society toward helping the injured.

This also was the beginning of a healthy relationship that developed between the village church and the big city Church. The big church caught the spirit of the village revival and her members began getting really serious about serving God. Some discovered that they didn't know God as their saviour and were *born again.* Many were made *pure in*

---

[42]Matt 5:7

heart and filled with the Spirit. Scores of people were *healed of physical diseases*, and a real Bible Pentecost began to prevail in the land.